BETTER THAN GOOD

LANE HAYES

Dreamspinner Press

Published by
Dreamspinner Press
5032 Capital Circle SW
Ste 2, PMB# 279
Tallahassee, FL 32305-7886
USA
http://www.dreamspinnerpress.com/

ISBN: 978-1-62380-639-2
Digital ISBN: 978-1-62380-640-8

Printed in the United States of America
First Edition
July 2013

For Bob, my love.

| 1 |

IT WAS early October. The clawing heat of a DC summer had finally given way to a glorious cool crisp autumn evening. I had been out with a big group of friends, which had dwindled to four as the night wore on. My friend Curt was one of the four, and he made a call for the remaining partiers to head over to Club Indigo in Dupont Circle. Curt was gay and was probably horny and ready to play. The rest of us were just tipsy enough to go along with him and have another drink or two before climbing into taxis to take us back across the river to Georgetown and our humble apartment near the university.

I'd been with Curt to clubs and gay bars on occasion. I just figured he was always willing to hang with us at sports bars and local straight haunts, so why not return the favor and keep him company? Besides, he was schnockered that night, and we agreed he needed adult supervision until we could persuade him to go home.

There was a small line at the club entrance. It felt invigorating to stand out in the cool autumn night and drink in the fresh air for a minute. I remember thinking it was a good thing the line was short or we would have set aside our kind intentions to keep Curt company. The atmosphere was definitely different in that part of town. It had a vibe all its own. And at one in the morning, the streets on and near the Circle belonged to the gays. Curt happily pointed out the leather daddies, twinks, and just plain hunky guys as we waited. I was amused, but I could tell Dave and Jason were uncomfortable and beginning to regret our impetuousness.

We paid the cover, and three of us headed toward the bar while Curt made a beeline for the main dance floor. The sound inside the club was deafening. The music had a jungle-like beat I could feel vibrate through my entire body. And the lights were a flashing display of color, making it difficult to focus unless you were inches away from whomever you were trying to get close to. A drink would help. I ordered a vodka soda and then made my way through the crowd to a short set of stairs leading to the dance floor below. I figured the height would allow me to scope out Curt while I waited for Dave and Jason to pick up our drinks.

Someone brushed past me in his effort to move from the bar area down to the main dance floor. He danced around me near the floor's edge as though he was trying to make his way toward center stage. There was something in the way he moved that caught my eye. He was liquid and sure in his movements, and I could see from the hot stares of the crowd around me that I wasn't the only one mesmerized. His hair was black in the dark club, but I couldn't clearly see what he looked like unless I moved down toward the main level. I looked back toward the bar and saw Dave hand signal that he was still waiting for the drinks. I gave him a brief nod and then found myself moving down the steps. I didn't intend to follow this guy, but I wanted to see his small, lithe body move up close.

I had lost him in the crowd of sweaty, scantily clad, sexy men gyrating to a Lady Gaga song, and was about to turn back to the bar when I caught sight of him a second time. The light was better where I stood, and as I got my first good look at him, my breath literally caught in my chest. I had never seen anyone, male or

2

female, so beautiful in my life. His hair was so dark it may as well have been black. He swung his hands above his head, and his long, straight bangs fell into his right eye as his head fell forward. His hips never stopped moving. He was wearing clothes meant to show his body to perfection: tight dark jeans and a tight fire-engine red V-neck T-shirt. He was much shorter than my own six one. I guessed him to be about five eight, tops. He seemed a bit on the thin side, but toned, as though he spent some time in the gym.

I watched as he opened his eyes and leaned in closer to hear something a boy dancing near him said. He smiled at the boy and then turned to look directly at me.

I swear the noise and vibrations of the club went suddenly silent. Men may have been dancing, talking, laughing above the din of the music, but in my head it was quiet. Crazy, right? He was still staring in my direction, but my feet wouldn't move. Should I be moving toward him, away from him? I was paralyzed. He made the decision for me. In an instant he was inches away from me, and I could see I had been completely correct. This guy was stunning.

I guess some backstory about me might be helpful. I was twenty-four and finishing law school at Georgetown while interning at a prestigious law firm downtown. I was hoping to be hired when I graduated in the spring next year. I had a great group of friends who were largely struggling students like me. All of us, for the most part, had great educations and were hopeful to find real jobs in a crappy economy.

Oh… and I had a girlfriend. I was straight. Didn't I mention that?

I couldn't remember ever feeling so drawn to anyone, though, and the partial truth was that I was more than half-drunk. So I decided to not question what it meant to be a straight guy dancing with a gay man. I decided go with the flow. This was something I could blame on Curt if it ever got thrown in my face. You're supposed to dance at dance clubs, and really, that was all I was doing. So what if the guy I was dancing with was smoking hot?

I didn't have any recriminating thoughts going through my head while we were dancing. I was truly mesmerized. I had never seen anyone who could move like this guy. He was seriously sexy. His hips never stopped, and his hands were in constant motion. I wondered, strangely, if he was a hand talker. I wondered what his voice sounded like. Now that I was so close to him, I could see he was of Latin decent, which made me wonder where he was from and if he spoke with an accent. I wondered how old he was and if he was attached. Geez, maybe his boyfriend was an old geezer who liked watching his hot young thing dance with other men, or maybe he was outside for a smoke and I was going to get my ass kicked when he returned and found me drooling over his guy. Sure, I would explain that I was straight, and he'd get a huge laugh at the straight guy who couldn't take his eyes off his lover.

I admit a lot of stupid thoughts crashed and collided in my head as we moved closely on the overcrowded dance floor. It was as though I could tell this first meeting was something out of the ordinary. I'd had those moments before, but never with a person. For instance, I remember receiving acceptance letters from Columbia and Georgetown Law Schools and knowing instinctively that Georgetown was where I would go. I was not a "go by the seat of your pants, let fate take you where it will" kind of a guy. I was a planner. A methodical planner at times. However, I'd learned to trust my gut.

As I did my best to not embarrass myself on the floor with my superior dance partner, I also tried to remind myself to stay in my buzz-addled happy place and to not overthink. This was just a lark. A bit of fun before finally heading home for the night and dealing with the inevitable hangover in the morning.

Our difference in height should have been awkward. I was easily five inches taller than him. Where he was slender and fine-boned, I was broad shouldered and built like the former college quarterback I was. However, I got the impression he could have danced with anyone and no one would notice his partner, no matter how good-looking they were. And although I knew I was considered better than average looking, he was extraordinary.

The lights dimmed and the beat slowed dramatically, but I caught my partner's incredible smile as he signaled me to follow him and made a get-a-drink motion. I kept close to him as we exited the floor without actually touching him, although I was very aware that my fingers itched to curl into his belt loops and draw my hand along the olive skin exposed just above his low-waisted jeans.

We made it to the main bar, and I watched him wiggle his way with a breathtaking smile or a gentle touch as he pushed through the three-person-deep line to make his way to the front and placed himself right in front of a bartender who was seemingly just delivering his last order. He looked back at me and smiled again. I gave him a little wave, but was suddenly feeling a bit silly. What was I doing? I took a minute to glance around the club, trying to spot my buddies in the mass of bodies. I guessed Curt was dancing, but I would have bet Dave and Jason were somewhere near the bar. I thought I spotted them but was distracted by a hand on my forearm.

"Hey. I didn't know what you drank, so I just got two kamikazes. Cheers!"

He leaned in to speak in my ear as he handed the glass over. No foreign accent, I mused. A nice voice, though, and a fucking heart-stopping smile. His eyes positively seemed to light up when he gave that beautiful smile, and although I couldn't ever remember noticing such a thing before, I wanted to tell him so. I wanted to say, "Wow, you have the nicest smile, you have the most gorgeous eyes, you must be the most beautiful man I've ever seen." Thankfully, I didn't embarrass myself quite that badly. Instead, I took the offered glass and returned his smile.

"Thanks. That was really nice of you."

Okay. That was lame. But I was practically tongue-tied. I didn't know what to say or how to act suddenly. It was like I was a freshman in high school trying to make time with a varsity cheerleader. Only the same-sex version. Luckily, he saved me.

"I haven't seen you here before. First time?"

"Yeah. You come here often?"

I did not just say that.

Oh boy. I needed to make an exit or be saved by one of my friends fast. I was a drowning man. I wanted to blame it on the alcohol, but I think I realized it was just me. I was really nervous. Ugh!

He didn't laugh at me, though. He just gave me a small grin and sipped his drink. I noticed the way his straight black hair fell into his eyes, and I felt a very real impulse to brush it away for him. I watched him swing his head back and use only his thumb to tame his bangs. Strangely, I found the movement graceful.

"Often enough, I guess. What's your name?"

"Matt. You?"

"Aaron."

"Nice to meet you, Aaron. Thank you for the drink."

"You're welcome. Don't be offended, but I have to ask. You seem a little out of your comfort zone.... Are you here on a bet?"

I think I almost spit up half my kamikaze, but I managed to swallow it at the last second. Nice save.

"Ha! Actually I'm here with some friends. Total free-willing participants. It's great here," I added, "just loud."

I know I am a former jock and probably look the type. I stay fit and eat right, for the most part. However, I'm not and never have been a stereotypical beer-guzzling, good-time party jock who probably got hit one too many times playing ball in college. I have a brain and can usually hold my end of a decent conversation. Why not tonight?

"Whoa! We have been looking for you, man!" Well, here was my escape. I could see Jason and Dave making their way from the other end of the packed bar toward Aaron and me.

Aaron noticed my buddies too. He looked over my right shoulder as they approached and then leaned up to say something in my left ear, gesturing at the same time for me to come down to his height.

"Nice to meet you, Matt."

And then he kissed my cheek and turned back toward the dance floor. I was shocked, which was a little silly, but I hadn't expected the kiss. I felt like I'd been cheated a bit. I wanted him to come back and do it again. Maybe this time I'd move my head and he'd catch my lips instead.

He quickly disappeared into the sea of gyrating bodies, thumping music, and flashing lights. I nodded to my friends, who I was sure hadn't seen the kiss, and followed them outside.

We gave a collective sigh as we breathed in the first bit of cool early morning DC air. It felt great to be outside after fighting the press of people inside the busy club.

"Hey, Matt, who's your boyfriend?" Dave teased. Jason was flagging down a taxi, but he heard Dave and had to add his own jab.

"Kinda hot, Matt. Should we warn Kristin she's got some competition?" Jason jeered.

"Ha-ha," I replied in my best deadpan voice. "Where's Curt? Are we leaving him here?"

"Said he found a hot date. Let's go. My buzz is fading, and I'd like to be back in hetero land before it's gone and I'm sober, wondering what the fuck I'm doing at a gay club on a Saturday night," Dave groused.

I barely remember the cab ride home, but the hangover I'd expected the following day did not disappoint. I'm fairly certain I woke up at noon, downed some aspirin, and chased it with a sports drink before I parked myself on my sofa in front of the big screen television to watch a day's worth of football. Dave and Curt were my roommates. They were in the same state as me, and we were likeminded in our quest for football, greasy food, and a little hair of the dog that afternoon. Jason lived nearby with his girlfriend, Chelsea. They were a serious couple. We all joked that Jase's night out with us had cost him the next day with both a hangover and a girl to nag at him about how much football a guy could possibly watch. Poor bastard.

I know there is an elephant in the room. I said I had a girlfriend. What was the deal?

Her name was Kristin. She was finishing her undergrad at Georgetown. We'd met about a year ago at a party somewhere near campus. Sweet, pretty, and not terribly demanding of my time, she was the perfect girlfriend for me. We called each other boyfriend and girlfriend, but I think it was almost more of an acknowledgement that we had barely any time for our classes, internships, and friends, let alone screwing around, even with each other. The sheer convenience of a date and sex when we were able to get together was probably the biggest reason we were together at all.

Don't get me wrong. I liked Kristin a lot, but I had no illusions of this being a life-changing relationship. I was not ready to pick out china patterns, and I really hoped she wasn't thinking along those lines either.

I was sprawled out on the sofa when Dave announced he could hear my phone. I begged him to bring it to me. It landed hard on my chest when he chucked it at me. I'd missed the call anyway. "Missed call from Kristin," the screen read. Hmm. I figured I'd deal with her later. I wasn't in the mood to chat in my current condition.

"Was that Kristin? Making sure you didn't bring any hot guys home last night?" Curt wiggled his eyebrows suggestively. "I meant for me, of course. But then I guess you'd just be helping out a friend, so she'd probably be cool with that, right?"

"I didn't think you needed any help, Curtster. We were all sound asleep when you finally made your way home," I reminded him.

"Yeah right. More like you were all passed out, asshole. I didn't stay much longer than you anyway."

He took a swig of beer from the bottle and then paused to give me an "I'm serious" look when he heard "mmm-hmm" in reply.

"Saw you dancing with a sexy boy, though." Curt's eyebrows were wiggling again. "That guy is seriously hot. I've seen him a few times around the Circle. He is fiiinnne. Did you get his name?"

"Well, I didn't ask him out or anything but yeah, we exchanged names."

"And?"

"What?"

"What's his name, jackass? Geez!"

"I don't remember. We just danced, as you well know. Or was I supposed to introduce you?" My voice had taken on a raspy quality indicative of too much fun the night before.

"Yes! Bad friend! I've explained my strategy to you dumb shits countless times. If I'm going to have straight so-called friends come to gay establishments with me, they should make themselves useful. I mean, you guys are all somewhat decent-looking, and if a hot guy like your new friend starts hitting on you, it is your duty as a good friend to set him straight, so to speak, and send him my way. Why do I need to remind you boys? I do the same for you when I'm out with you guys. Girls love gay boys."

"Sorry. My bad. Don't get your panties in a twist. We just danced. It's not like I was 'getting to know him'." I threw air quotes around the last part just to annoy Curt.

"You danced for a while, though," Curt mused.

"He's right," Dave agreed. He brought a fresh round of beers with him. I took one and closed my eyes. I was just starting to feel human again.

"Right about what exactly? We danced. It's a dance club. End of story. Next time I'll get numbers for you. 'Kay? Now shut up and watch the game."

"Hmm. Okay, big guy. Whatever you say." Curt seemed to be placating me, but I was just happy he agreed to move on.

I don't know why I didn't tell Curt the truth. Aaron. Of course I remembered his name. All I could think of was Aaron. It baffled me. It really had been the most casual of experiences, just as I'd told my friends. No big deal. So why, when I should be thinking about my classes tomorrow and even answering my cell when my girlfriend called, was I thinking about Aaron at all? I didn't have any answers, and I wasn't sure my head was clear yet anyway, so I decided to put off thinking of any sort for the rest of the day.

A WEEK later, I still found myself thinking about him. I was replaying the moment we first caught each other's eye and everything went quiet in my mind. It seemed like a sign or something. And these constant thoughts made me wonder about him. Where was he from? Where did he work? Was he with anyone? My sudden obsession didn't make sense. Maybe I really just needed to get laid. I hadn't seen Kristin at all that week, although we talked a little. Maybe I was just horny, and thinking about the last hot person I'd been around was doing something to me. The fact that it was a man instead of a woman didn't bother me nearly as much as I would have thought.

The following Saturday, I walked up to Kristin's townhouse to pick her up for a date. I put more effort into my appearance than I normally would have. I gelled my wavy dark-blond hair, which probably could have used a cut, and wore a blue button-down shirt

Kristin said matched my eyes. It had been a while and I was worried about my blue balls. Kristin and I didn't have the type of relationship where we could just say what we wanted. We were polite to one another. It was old-fashioned, but she was pretty conservative, so I figured this was how she wanted it. We'd make a date a few days ahead of time, have a nice dinner and sometimes go to a movie, and then have sex, usually back at her place. The sex was nice. Not earth-shattering, but somewhat regular, so I didn't mind. I didn't spend the night often. Neither of us seemed interested in the overnight thing anyway. I guess that night I was hoping whatever happened between Kristin and me would keep me from thinking anymore about Aaron.

Kristin opened the door before I had a chance to knock. She was dressed in tight jeans with high-heeled black boots and a long orange sweater that complemented her honey-colored hair. She looked stylish and beautiful. And she looked happy to see me.

"Hey there, stranger." She reached out to touch my hand, and I moved the rest of the way in to kiss her softly on her lips. She seemed to have a lot of gloss or something on, and I didn't want to taste it on my own lips for the next hour.

"How are you? Hungry? I was thinking maybe we could try that new Italian place on M Street. I made a reservation, but if you feel like something else, that's cool too."

I was doing my best to accommodate my date. She never told me what she felt like eating. Ever. It was probably something she didn't realize she did, but when it came to food, whether it was take home or out for a meal, Kristin always deferred to me. I'd come to realize that if I didn't want to play the "I don't care, what do you feel like?" game when we went out, I needed to take matters into my own hands. She never disagreed about the places I chose either. You would think that I loved this easygoing culinary attitude, but honestly I felt like I was walking on eggshells. I would actually have preferred she give an honest opinion, so I was not solely responsible for food choices. She had plenty of other opinions, but for whatever reason she was never willing to share her dining preferences with me. Weird.

"Sounds great. Let me grab my bag. I'm ready to go."

She joined me on the sidewalk outside her place a few minutes later and reached out to hold my hand. My car key was in that hand, though, so we did a clumsy dance as the key pinched her skin and her giant bag (with God only knows what in it) fell from her other arm, and I finally clued in that I was the cause. We both gave an awkward laugh and tried again. This already felt difficult. Why couldn't this be uncomplicated? As in "we haven't seen each other all week, let's do it first and then worry about the rest"? I sound like a caveman, I know, but I was beginning to get a sinking feeling that, even if the evening went the way I thought it would, I still wouldn't be getting Aaron out of my head tonight.

The quick recap went as follows: dinner, back to Kristin's place for a drink, and yes, sex. A nice night, sure, but I was on my way home before eleven and not at all ready for bed. I called Curt at the last minute before I turned onto our street to see where everyone was. Curt answered on the third ring.

"Yell-oo!" Curt sounded a little gone and was obviously in a very loud bar. A gay bar? Only one way to find out.

"Where are you? Is Dave out with you?"

"No, he had a date. How did yours go? Couldn't have been that great if you're calling me before midnight. I hope you at least got some." He didn't sound drunk anymore at all. Just annoying. And truthfully, part of me had been hoping to go save him and run into Aaron again while I was at it.

"Where are you? You need my mad straight-guy skills to help land you a little nookie?"

"You are such a kind and thoughtful friend, Matt. I'm at the Zodiac Bar. I don't need your so-called straight-guy skills, but come join us anyway."

He hung up before I could ask whom he was with. Some of his gay friends are really cool and some are just not. Whatever. One drink I could handle, and it would keep me from going home to an empty apartment or having to listen to Dave and his date going at it if the apartment wasn't empty after all. Yeah, the Zodiac was sounding better by the second.

The Zodiac Bar was a cool little gay-friendly pub in the city off of Logan. It was on a quieter street and on the small side, but it was pretty hip inside. Very sleek and trendy, with a huge fireplace lit with colored glass rocks and small ottomans used as moveable seats on one end, and a gorgeous glass bar with cool backlights just opposite. I checked my reflection before I walked in, and figured the khakis and button-down shirt would do. I wasn't looking for a date, just a drink, I reminded myself.

I spotted Curt at a small corner table with two other guys who I think were named Randy and Dan. I nodded in his direction and then headed for the bar for my much-needed drink. Of course he was with Randy and Dan. They were cool but kind of camp. I needed a liquid equalizer. I ordered a vodka tonic from an extraordinarily good-looking bartender. I heard the patron next to me give a small laugh as my arm was gently jostled.

"Yeah, he's hot, alright."

"Uh, hey…," I stammered. It was Aaron.

What were the odds that the one person I'd been thinking about for an entire week and figured I'd probably never see again was standing next to me? I felt suddenly warm all over and had a very real fear I wouldn't be able to articulate an intelligent thought. I didn't understand my attraction to this guy.

He looked from the bartender back to me, and recognition dawned across his face.

"We danced last week, right? We met. How funny." He shifted his body so he fully faced me and gave me a good once over. "I forgot your name. I'm sorry. I'm Aaron."

"Matt."

"Oh yes. Matt. Matt, who looked like he lost a bet Matt. And here you are a week later in—" He did a dramatic side-to-side glance around the bar, his hands gesturing alongside. "—yep, a gay bar. Maybe you weren't coerced after all, Matt?"

His face was so beautiful, and his eyes were twinkling to let me know he was teasing me. I once again found myself under his spell and belatedly aware that he was waiting for me to speak. Somehow I found my voice, although I had to clear my throat before the words would come.

"I'm here with a friend. Actually, the same friend I was with last week at the club too."

He rolled his eyes but smiled again.

"I owe you a drink. What would you like?" I was scrambling, hoping to keep him talking to me. He considered me for a minute before answering.

"Alright. I'll have a cosmo, please."

The gorgeous bartender appeared, and just as I was about to place Aaron's order, he leaned across the counter and grabbed Aaron lightly by his collar. Aaron met him midway and they kissed. Not a passionate lover-like kiss, but a more-than-friends kind of kiss.

"JoJo, honey, this nice guy is buying me a cosmo. Heavy on the good stuff, please." Aaron batted his eyelashes at the tall, dark, handsome, and super-muscular bartender. They would look good together, I mused. JoJo, or Joe probably, set my drink in front of me with a wink.

"Sure thing, babe." Joe gave Aaron a bit of a lecherous look before he stepped away to make the cocktail.

"Your boyfriend?" I couldn't help asking.

Aaron giggled, his eyes still twinkling.

"No. I don't have a boyfriend. JoJo is a flirt. Luckily his boyfriend knows that."

I figured I probably shouldn't ask any other Joe-the-bartender questions. I was confused enough as it was.

"I'm going to guess you have a girlfriend, though. Am I right?" Aaron's eyes were now lit with challenge, as if to say, "Don't lie, I'll know the truth anyway." I stalled for a minute, taking a drink of my vodka.

"Yeah, sort of. I mean, we aren't serious, but yeah, I guess." Poor Kristin. I was sure she'd love to hear the ringing endorsement I was giving us, especially since I'd just been in her bed a couple hours ago. What a dick. What was my problem?

"Nice. I'd love to hear her side. I bet she's all in looove. Are you one of those curious guys? Want to know if you might, just maybe, could possibly like cock and probably should give it a try before you get hitched and move out to the suburbs to start a family? Maybe just get it out of your system?" He was deliberately taunting me now. And it was working.

"Down, boy," Joe admonished Aaron as he set his drink down. "Leave the poor guy alone. He's just buying a drink, not a house in the country."

"Sorry. You're right. I'm rude. What's new? Oops, you don't know me. I'll try to be good, starting now. So… tell me, Matt, what's your story? Are you a student, a young business type, a politician in training? Where are you from, how old are you, what is your last name, your favorite color, what do you like doing in your spare time, which suburb do you see yourself moving to when you finally do settle down with your girl, and how many kids will you have?"

Aaron finally stopped talking long enough to take a drink of his cosmo, and then he gave me an expectant look when I didn't respond immediately to his barrage of questions.

"Okay. Let's see. I'll tell you my story if you tell me yours. Agreed?" When Aaron nodded in agreement, I went on. "Well, you packed a lot of questions in there. Let me know if I miss something.

"I'm finishing my law degree at Georgetown and am interning with Lawton, Hughes, Banks, and Kelleford. It looks like I will have a position with them when I graduate, too, which is beyond amazing to me. I'm from Pittsburgh originally, my family is all there and it's home, but I like the energy here. I'm not moving back anytime soon or probably ever. I'm twenty-four. My last name is Sullivan. Favorite color? Hmm, I guess blue." I paused when I heard Aaron snort and mumble "original." I raised my eyebrows.

He gestured with his hands. "Go on, I'm on the edge of my seat. Don't stop now."

"Well, since you're so interested, I will. Let's see, where was I?"

"Hobbies and settling down with your new wife, I think," Aaron suggested innocently.

"Well, I love sports. Especially football, baseball, and basketball. But my real passion is music. I play guitar. Actually, there's a bar by the college where I play once in a while with a friend of mine just for fun. And as for the last question, smartass... I don't see myself settling down in the suburbs anytime soon. I'm not marrying anyone anytime soon either. I'd love to have kids someday, yeah, but who knows how many? I imagine my partner will want some say in that number too. Your turn."

"Very nice, Mr. Sullivan. I'd love to reciprocate, but it looks like your friend, or just someone who desperately wants your attention, is waving at you."

Sure enough, Curt was on his feet, waving in my direction. I didn't want to break this contact with Aaron, so I waved at Curt but made no motion to join him at the table. Of course he came to the bar instead. I introduced him to Aaron. He looked so funny with his curiosity plain as day on his face. I loved keeping him in suspense, but even if I was inclined to share, I wouldn't know what to say. "Don't mind me, Curt, I'm just trying to make some time with Aaron here" would probably do the job, but I wasn't quite sure about what I was doing.

"Hey, we're heading to Tango to meet up with one of Randy's work buddies. You coming with?" Curt asked.

"You go on. I'll meet you over there." I didn't think my response through, I just went with what I wanted. And I wanted to talk to Aaron.

Curt gave me a short nod with a funny look I couldn't quite read but was sure I'd hear all about later. "Okay, then. Nice meeting you, Aaron."

"You too," Aaron replied politely. He waited until Curt was out of earshot and then turned back to me.

"I'm very curious about you, straight boy. Why are you here with me? Or—" He paused with dramatic effect. "—are you curious and not so straight? Hmm." He turned quickly and began to walk away. "Let's go take their table. I'll answer all your questions if you're still interested in moi." I found myself staring at his back with my mouth open. Rendered speechless again.

I followed him to Curt's vacant table in time to overhear Aaron wheeling and dealing with another patron for first rights to sit. The bar was getting busier and this looked to be the last empty and somewhat private table.

"I'm so sorry, doll. Our friends were just leaving this table for us. Did you see them? They should have stayed till we got our drinks sorted, but they were in such a hurry!"

"I was here first" was the unimpressed reply from a bored-looking young hipster.

"Not really," Aaron insisted stubbornly.

"It's cool. We can go back to the bar." I didn't want to get in an argument with a stranger over a table he'd obviously gotten to first.

Aaron gave me a fierce scowl. Actually, it just made him look adorable, but I'm sure the message was for me to keep quiet and let him handle the situation.

"My boyfriend was just explaining to me that he thinks he's bi and I'm trying to cope. I can't cope at the bar. I need this table." Aaron's eyes filled and the guy looked alarmed.

"Whoa, don't cry. You take it." The stranger gave Aaron a sympathetic parting glance before turning to glare at me. "Asshole."

"Hey!" I was offended. And boyfriend? I looked down at Aaron, who was now happily perched on a stool at the much sought-after table. He looked positively smug. And adorable. I sighed and took a seat.

"Really? You wanted the table that badly?"

"Yep. My feet are killing me and there was only one of him and two of us. He should thank us. He'll meet more potential beaus at the bar, not sitting here in the dark. He was practically being a wallflower!" Aaron's hands were flying a mile a minute as he shared his convoluted logic with me.

"You are devious." I had to laugh out loud at the very self-satisfied expression on his face. It was much darker at this table than it had been at the bar. A single votive lit his face. The candlelight suited him. "I guess you have a story to tell now. Your turn," I prompted.

"I can't remember the questions, remind me, or better yet, just ask me new ones. Much more exciting that way."

"Okay. Um, let's see. What do you do? I mean for a living? Where were you born? How long have you lived here? What nationality are you? Brothers or sisters? What's your favorite band or singer? Favorite TV show? Um, I can't think of anything else. Go ahead. Answer away." I leaned back and noticed him watching me intently. His bangs fell into his eye again, and my fingers yearned to touch him. Talking was better. "Well? I answered yours. Your turn."

"I have a quirky memory, but I'll do my best here." He gave an exaggerated cough and began. "I work as an editorial assistant at a fashion mag. You didn't ask but I love fashion. Specifically fashion photography. I try to get my editor to loan me out to our lead photographers to assist them when it's slow in her office."

"So you want to be a photographer?" I interrupted. That sounded very interesting and for some reason, I wanted to know why.

"Yes. I do it as a hobby for now because I need to pay the rent, so for the time being, that's all it can be. I'm trying to build a portfolio, but it's just a work in progress at this point. So… now that I'm completely distracted, what exactly was the next question?"

"What do you like about photography? If you could make a living at it, would you want to freelance or what? I'm interested." Aaron gave me a dubious look. "Really," I assured him, "tell me."

"I love that a moment is captured and a story can be told all with one single shot. If a photographer is truly great, you want to go back time and again to look at that photo and see what you may have missed after the first peek. I would love to be sought after and unique enough that I could freelance at a high level. But that's a dream, Matty. Bills must be paid. And stop interrupting me. I'll be talking about me all night if you're not careful. You'll be bored to tears, asleep on this very popular table, and if anyone I know comes by, I'll never live it down. 'Aaron talks guy into catatonic state.' I can hear them now." I noticed, as he wound himself up at the end with his little speech, that his hands were moving at record speed and his effeminate vocal affectation went up several notches. I guessed I'd caught him off guard asking about something he was passionate about. Interesting.

"Matty? You called me Matty." I gave him my best annoyed expression and saw Aaron's shoulders visibly shift downward. He was relaxed again, and I was inordinately pleased with myself. "Okay, Aaron, please continue. But first tell me, what's your last name?"

"Mendez. And I'm Puerto Rican. I believe that was one of your questions. Full-blooded. Both parents from there and *sí, yo hablo español.*" He gave me a very Americanized Spanish accent, but I would bet his Spanish was impeccable.

"Were you born there? In Puerto Rico?"

"No. I'm from a little town outside Baltimore called Ellicott. Almost local. It's just an hour away. Forty-five minutes if there isn't a smidge of traffic. My parents were both born in PR, though. My mom came over when she was really little and my father was in his early twenties. He learned to speak English when he was younger, but his accent is still pretty thick."

"Siblings?"

"Three. Two older sisters, Maria and Tess, and a younger brother, Paul. And moving on and away from family fun… I love *Project Runway*, Heidi is adorable, but honestly I think Nina is my favorite. I love people who say it like it is, you know? And I love *America's Next Top Model*. Tyra is great, right?"

Huh? I didn't know. I had lost him at Project something, and I didn't know who Heidi and Nina were. I thought he said his sisters were Maria and Tess.

"I'm not sure about that, but let's stay on track. I think we move onto music. Who is your favorite band or your favorite singer?" I asked.

"I'm a huge Gaga fan. And I love Rihanna! Oh, and Adele too. And…."

Our tastes in music were polar opposite; however, music was a subject I could discuss for hours. And before I knew it, we had done just that. We talked about music in movies and television. Jazz music, American standards, commercial jingles, and even musicals. Aaron seemed to know a little bit about most genres and was passionate about those he liked the best. His enthusiasm was contagious. He was easy company and the time flew. A quick look at my watch told me it was after 2:00 a.m. The bar would be offering last call soon. I needed to get home. I had a ton of work to do for school next week. But I was reluctant to leave my new friend.

"Whoa! I had no idea it was so late. I should get going. Can I give you a lift home? Do you live nearby?"

Aaron smiled a little tiredly.

"No, I'm good. I live close. I feel like a short walk."

"I'm not letting you walk home alone in the middle of the night. Let me take you home. Just drop you off, okay?"

"Well, since you're being so chivalrous, I shouldn't refuse. Thanks."

We headed out of the still-packed bar and into the cool early morning air. It felt great, and I had to admit *I* felt great. I had honestly enjoyed just talking with Aaron. He was funny, interesting, and very intelligent. Our conversation ranged from music to movies to politics. I was more than a little sorry for our time together to end.

We walked the short distance to my car in silence, and he gave me directions to his place, which definitely was very nearby. I still felt better taking him home at this time of night/morning. The radio was on. Aaron heard the classic rock tune and scoffed.

"Yuck." He changed it to a techno-sounding song. "Better," he said and started to hum along. I should have been really irritated by his over familiarity, but I found myself mildly intrigued with his force of personality. And I could handle the techno crap for a two-minute drive.

"Thank you, thank you, kind sir. Here is my humble abode. I'm much too tired to invite you up, and I'm not that kind of girl. Actually, scratch that last part. But I am tired. It's been great hanging out with you, Matty. See you around."

He blew an air kiss in my direction and turned to open the car door. I stopped him with a hand on his shoulder. He turned back to face me, and suddenly we were much closer than we had been since our first dance at the club. Our eyes met, and I moved in closer still. I noticed for the first time that he was wearing eyeliner. His eyes were beautiful either way. They were a true hazel, and even in the darkened car interior, I could see the flecks of brown and green.

He moved the smallest bit closer and our lips touched. Our eyes were still open, and our lips just touched. The air suddenly felt electric in the small car. One of us moaned, and that was it. Our lips sealed in a true kiss, our eyes closed, and I moved my left arm to bring him closer to me. I needed to touch him. He licked over my bottom lip. My whole body reacted as I opened my lips to let him in. Our tongues danced and swirled. It was frenzied and passionate, like nothing I'd felt kissing anyone ever. My hands moved over his face and through his dark hair. It was soft to the touch. I shifted my hands to the nape of his neck to hold him closer as I deepened the kiss. He groaned into my mouth, and I could feel it throughout my body. I was more turned-on than even a hot kiss should call for. And it ended too soon. He pulled away from me and gently pushed me back.

"Wow, Matty. That was some good night kiss." Aaron let out an exaggerated sigh and once again reached for the door handle. "I'll see you around."

"Can I get your number?" I held my breath for a second. I wanted him to want to see me again too. But I had no idea what I was thinking. To what end?

"Matt." He paused and looked into my eyes. "Why? I'm not sure if it was apparent to you or not, but I'm gay. I'm out, I'm proud. You are maybe iffy about the gay part, bi, or just curious, I don't know. But you aren't out or proud. And you told me you have a girlfriend. I don't know why you want my number. I like you and I loved just talking to you tonight, but really."

"Aaron." I had to try one more time. "Please. I don't know what the hell I'm doing here. I admit it. I've been thinking about you nonstop for a week. And somehow I run into you again tonight. We spend the evening talking. Look, I don't know why, but I'm...." I couldn't think of anything else to say. Frustration was eating at me. It was silent in the car for a minute, just the sound of us breathing.

Aaron sighed heavily again.

"Okay. Give me your phone number and I'll call you so you have it in your received calls. Good? But Matt...." He paused and looked into my eyes with a very serious expression. "I'm not playing games. You're hot and you seem like a good guy. Against my better judgment, I like you. But you have baggage, my friend. And I prefer to travel lightly."

He took my number and called it from his cell. Then he looked at me meaningfully before getting out of the car.

"Good night, Matty. Take care."

I leaned across the center partition and watched as he opened the door to his apartment building. Once he was safely inside, I sat back in my seat and put my head on the steering wheel. I let the waves of confusion and frustration wash over me before I pulled slowly away from the curb.

| 2 |

THE month that followed passed quickly. I didn't see Aaron. I didn't try to call him. I didn't regret anything that had gone on between us. It really was innocent enough, with one minor exception. Aaron was a man. A beautiful, sexy gay man. And I identified myself as a heterosexual and had a girlfriend.

Here was the truth... I wasn't completely straight, which I suppose meant I was bisexual. What I hated was that I had to qualify what I meant by that statement. I had found other men attractive in the past; however, I only acted on it once.

I was a freshman in college at a very raucous party when I met my one and only previous gay experience. But it was a doozy. I didn't know the guy at all. I think he was a little older than me. I remember us talking in the kitchen and then him being literally in my space. It didn't bother me. I remember being turned on. So when he told me he wanted to show me something in the bedroom, I followed him. I wasn't thinking sex. I was thinking he was going to offer me drugs, which I would have refused. But I didn't predict the searing-hot kiss or the way his hands moved all over my body. I couldn't have predicted my body's response. I just went with it.

When he fumbled with my belt and unzipped my jeans, I just went with it. When he slipped his hands under my briefs and kneaded my ass with strong, sure hands, I sighed and pushed forward. When he cupped my balls and my dick, my breath caught, but I still went with it. I remember he was suddenly urgent as he stroked me. His grip was tight and felt amazing. I didn't think I'd last long. But he pulled away from me, taking something out of his pocket before shucking off his jeans and shoes. I literally stood there with my very hard dick in my hands, watching as he walked toward the bed and then placed a condom and packet of lube by his knees as he arranged himself on his hands and knees in front of me. His ass on full display. I remember he seemed breathy as he told me to fuck him.

I don't remember thinking beyond desire at that moment. I'd never done any of the things I'd done with him before. I was a homo virgin. I'd had sex with a couple of girlfriends in high school, but I was well aware that I was crossing into new territory. That was all the thinking I let my head do as I slipped the condom on, lubed up, and reached for him. We fucked. It was hot, tight, sweaty, and yeah, I liked it. A lot. Looking back at it, I'm sure I was a lousy lay. I think he knew enough to take care of himself. I couldn't think beyond my own primitive urges. We didn't linger after the act. I didn't feel ashamed at all, but I definitely felt confused.

In the six years since that experience, I had never seriously looked twice at a man until Aaron. Until Aaron, I had convinced myself that was a one-off drunken experience. One I owned but doubted I'd ever do again. Aaron and I hadn't done anything sexual, really. We had kissed. That's it. And now one month had gone by since that kiss, and all I could do was think of him.

I was very busy with classes and with my internship at the law firm. I'd played guitar and sang at the bar I had told Aaron about a couple of times. I'd watched my fair share of football with my friends, and yeah, I managed to spend some time with my girlfriend. But none of this stopped me from thinking of Aaron, wondering if

I'd bump into him at the market, at a coffee shop, or even on the street. I was thinking I should just give into the urge I had to call him. Then one day something happened to make me think I needed to do something sooner rather than later if I was going to get my sense of balance back.

It was a late Saturday afternoon in mid-November, so naturally I was parked in front of our large-screen TV watching college football with my buddies. Empty beer bottles and bags of chips were strewn about. The games hadn't been particularly exciting that day, but it didn't stop us from screaming at the television and one another with mostly good-natured jibes. I loved hanging out with my friends. I loved being with a bunch of guys sharing a beer or two and debating sports, politics, and current events. It was times like this that kept me from thinking about Aaron, which was a topic I didn't want to share with anyone. Not even Curt, who strangely enough hadn't brought up Aaron once since the day after I'd introduced them at the bar last month. Curt had asked me how my "friend" was the next day, made a comment regarding his hotness ("sizzling," I believe he said), and that was it. Not a word since. I was relieved.

There was a banging at the front door, and Jason got up off the ratty old sofa to answer. I gave a quick glance toward the door but was otherwise engrossed in the action on the screen. A double take had me groaning inside but plastering a fake smile on my face. It was Kristin with Chelsea, Jason's girlfriend, and Jen, a friend of Kristin's who was crushing on Dave. They walked into the apartment with grocery bags in hand.

"We're here to cook! Man cannot live on chips and beer alone!" Chelsea declared.

"How about spaghetti, boys? Garlic bread? A Caesar salad?" Kristin asked sweetly. She gave a shy smile aimed in my direction. I tried to return it and hoped it didn't look like a grimace. I wasn't happy with the new development.

I looked around at my buddies to see what they were thinking and found no support. Jason had his tongue down Chelsea's throat, and Dave had a stupid smile on his face. He looked genuinely pleased to see Jen. That left me staring at my girlfriend like an idiot. I needed to get up off the sofa and act like I was grateful she had come with reinforcement to save us from another weekend of eating pizza in front of the big screen.

I looked over at Curt, who had greeted the girls when they walked in but had since turned all his attention to his phone. I could tell he was not going to stay for dinner with three couples. Since I wasn't getting out of it, I needed to get up off my ass and say something to Kristin. "Why are you here?" probably wasn't the right thing to say, although it was all I could think.

She didn't seem to notice any awkwardness from me. In fact, she just gave me a quick kiss on the cheek and set to work in the cramped kitchen. I grabbed a beer and headed back to the living area, but not before I heard Chelsea say, "Kristin, are you making those Italian wedding meatballs too? Those are so yum!" I choked on my drink and scurried as quickly as possible back to the men and the game.

The rest of the evening was my own personal nightmare. Three couples, one obviously serious, one more casual (at least that was my take on Kristin and me), and one in the just-getting-to-know-each-other stage. And conversation centered around marriage. Ugh! How old did you want to be? Did you want a big or small wedding? What did you think about eloping? Like I said, hell. To be fair, the reason the conversation came up was that mutual friends of ours had just become engaged. They'd been dating for two years and he'd just popped the question. It still smelled a little bit like a setup to me. Maybe I was paranoid, but I felt like the girls were all testing the waters to see what the guy reaction to marriage and settling down was like. I was painfully silent. I was afraid to even look at Kristin. She didn't really think we were heading that way, did she?

Apparently, she did. She was telling a story about some friend of hers whose wedding we went to in the spring and commenting on how gorgeous the flowers were. Next she was onto bridesmaid dresses. What colors look good in what season? Seriously. The conversation was bad enough, but the surreptitious looks she cast in my direction made me feel a little queasy.

I liked Kristin, but marriage? I guess she'd make a good wife if I were ready for that kind of commitment. Let me be clear that I was not. Someday, sure, but honestly, I didn't think I felt like Kristin and I would really make it in the long run. We talked easily, we'd never had a real argument, and the sex was nice. But that's it. There was no passion. I admit it. I felt more passionate about the game she interrupted by bringing over dinner than I did about seeing her and being with her. If anything, I felt annoyed.

Hypothetically speaking, if we were to marry, it would be a polite kind of affair. I could see my life ten years from now when I was approaching my midthirties with my pretty wife, our two kids, and a dog living in the suburbs. I'd be a soccer dad on the weekends, and she'd be the perfect mom, involved in the kids' school and attending yoga and Pilates in her spare time. Maybe I would come to love her in time, but maybe I was just being a selfish bastard. If we had different ideas about where this relationship was heading, one of us should say something. Did it have to be me? Maybe I misread her wistful expression after all.

The girls insisted on cleaning up, although Dave stayed to chat Jen up and dry dishes. He must have had a bigger crush than I realized. When they came to join us in front of the television, the games had wound down for the night and someone had turned on a movie. A romantic comedy, of course. I could not catch a break! Couples had drifted to cuddle up with one another. I was sitting on my corner of the sofa when Kristin came to sit beside me. I put my arm around her, and I don't know why, but I hoped that would be all for the night. I didn't want to kiss her, hold her, and I didn't want sex. I just didn't feel it. I guess the wedding talk had scared me off more than I thought. Or maybe I was thinking of someone else.

I was desperate for this not to turn completely awkward, so I suggested we all go out for a drink. Dave and Jen politely declined and then made their way to Dave's room. Great. Now I definitely wanted out of the apartment. I didn't want to listen to those two going at it all night. I tried to give Jason a pleading look, which he pointedly ignored.

"No, man. Come on, Chels. Let's head back home. See ya, Matt. Bye, Kristin. And thanks for dinner." Jason had his coat in one hand and the other all over Chelsea's ass. Great. That left Kristin and me.

"Want to go out for a drink? Sam Thompson is supposed to be playing at that little bar off Pennsylvania," I asked her hopefully. I felt her tense up in my arms and realized I was playing this all wrong. Unfortunately I didn't think making it right would do either of us any good.

"Actually, I'm a little tired, Matt." We both turned toward the bedrooms as the first squeak of the box springs was heard. I raised my eyebrows and she gave me a faint smile in return.

"Mind taking me home?"

"Sure thing."

Kristin lived with two other roommates about ten minutes from my place. I knew she'd invite me in, and I was trying to find the least hurtful way to leave her and head into town. Maybe I'd call Curt and see where he'd gone. But Kristin knew me well enough to know I wouldn't want to go home with Dave and Jen doing the nasty back at my place. This was going to be tricky.

Help came in the form of her roommate, Stephanie. She was dressed in pajama bottoms and a tight T-shirt, no bra, eating ice cream straight from the container in front of what looked like yet another chick flick. This one looked like the sad kind, though. One look at Stephanie told me she was an emotional mess; tears were streaming down her face. Kristin rushed over to her side.

"Steph, what is it? What's wrong?"

"Men suck. I want to be a lesbian," she cried. Stephanie is actually a very pretty girl, but her eyes were puffy and red, and she looked a little miserable. I didn't really want to stick around to find out who had stood her up or let her down. I got that it was one of my gender. I didn't need to know any more.

"Um. Maybe I should head out, Kristin...." I was already backing up toward the front door.

"Yeah, I'm so sorry, Matt." She had her arm around Stephanie. She blew me a kiss over her sobbing friend's shoulder. I smiled and gave her a small wave as I made a mad dash for the door.

I breathed a sigh of immense relief as I stepped out into the cool November evening. It was still early. I knew I wasn't going home. I pulled out my cell and called Curt's number. I got his voice mail. There were other friends I could call, or I could just grab a beer on my own. But I couldn't stop thinking of Aaron. It had been almost a month. Would he even remember me? I pushed "send" before I could talk myself out of it.

The call was answered on the first ring, but it didn't sound like Aaron.

"Chel-lo... Aaron's phone...." The voice was masculine but lilting. It was very loud in the background. I'd bet Aaron and whoever had his phone were at a club. "I'm sure you're looking for Aaron, because I am too. I need to give him his phone." He must have pulled the phone just away from his mouth, but he was still yelling in my ear, "Yoo-hoo, Aaron honey... you just got a call. Yes, I answered it. You didn't say I shouldn't! Sorry... I don't know who it is. No wait, it said Matty. Who is Matty?"

I had to smile. Matty? I didn't mind it so much coming from Aaron.

"Matty, hold on. He's on his way, although he looks like he wants to strangle me. Be nice to him. He's a little cranky," Aaron's friend whispered loudly into the phone.

"I'm not cranky, bitch. Give me the phone, sweetie." That voice I'd know anywhere.

"Bitch, sweetie… which one is it, Aar Bear?"

"Hello?"

"Aar Bear? Hi, Aaron. It's me. Matt. I'm not sure if you remember…," I began nervously.

"Call me Aar Bear again and I'll hurt you, but don't be silly, of course I remember you, Matty. It's been a while. How are you?" Aaron's voice was like honey. I wanted to keep him talking, but moreover, I really wanted to see him.

"It has. I wanted to call you, but I wasn't sure I should. How've you been?"

"Same ol', same ol'… nothing exciting." He sounded great and anything but same ol' and unexciting to me.

"Can I see you, Aaron? I don't mean to sound weird, pathetic, whatever. I just… I can't stop thinking about you. What are you doing?"

I heard a small laugh, and Aaron said, "Yeah, Matt, that sounds good. I'm at a party, but I'm really ready to leave. Want to pick me up now?"

He gave me quick directions to a residence off of Logan. I had been sitting in my car while talking to Aaron, so I turned the engine on and headed over the bridge toward the Circle. Fifteen minutes later, I pulled up to the address Aaron had given me to find him standing outside with his arms wrapped around himself to ward off the chill. He saw my car and made his way to me.

"Where's your jacket?" I asked. He looked at me in surprise and then laughed.

"Matty, I didn't want to mess up my ensemble by covering it! Like the shirt?" I nodded slowly. Aaron had on a tight-fitted, floral-printed button-down shirt, which at least had long sleeves, and tight dark jeans. Yeah, he looked good. Really good.

"Yes, I like your shirt. You look amazing. But you look cold too. Want my coat?" I offered my coat almost without realizing I had done it. He looked surprised again, but he gave me that glorious smile and shook his head.

"No, I'm good. Thank you for offering. Where should we go?"

"Well, I have a suggestion, but if you'd rather go somewhere else, that's cool too," I began lamely.

He raised his eyebrows, inviting me to continue.

"This friend of mine, Sam, is playing at this little bar off Pennsylvania. It's pretty cool. A little crowded, but...."

"Sure. I'm in. Show me how the other half lives, Matty." I must have given him a funny look because he continued, "The straight half, I mean. This is a hetero bar you're taking me to, yes? I'm game and I promise not to embarrass you. Much." He said the last part tongue-in-cheek, but I still wondered what that was supposed to mean. Maybe he was referring to his tightly fitted clothes and the ever-present eyeliner. I guess he looked gay, but plenty of gay people went to straight bars, and vice versa. He was my friend. Who cared what anyone thought? I didn't imagine they'd think anything one way or the other. This was DC, not some backwater hick town.

The traffic was a little heavy the closer we got to the bar, so I parked in the first available spot I saw and suggested we walk the remaining two blocks.

"Aaron, seriously. You're going to freeze. Take my jacket. Please." He was wrapped around himself as closely as he could manage, but the guy was very lean. Of course he was cold. I took off my leather jacket and practically shoved it at him. He looked at me funny but didn't argue this time. The jacket was enormous on him. I had him by five inches easily and a good thirty pounds.

"I must look ridiculous!" He laughed out loud.

"Ridiculous but warm, and right now, which would you rather be? Come on, we're heading this way." I directed him up the avenue.

Along the way, he chatted nonstop about the party he'd just been to. A work gathering. Someone's birthday. He was supposed to go to his best friend Jay's house later, but he'd just text him and tell him he had other last-minute plans. He told me about a new layout he was helping the photographer with for his magazine shoot. And on and on. It was enchanting, honestly. I got the sense that things were never dull in Aaron's world. He wouldn't let them be. He asked about me, but I was able to give him only the briefest of updates before we were at our destination.

The bar was packed. It was wall-to-wall people. I signaled for him to follow me and made my way to the bar.

"What do you want?" I yelled above the din.

"Umm... let's see. A cosmo, please."

"Aaron. This is a *bar* bar. How about a vodka soda or vodka cranberry?"

"Really? They can't throw in a little triple sec and lime juice? Fine. I'll have a vodka cranberry, then. But make it strong. I was at a work party. I've had like two sips of wine tonight, and now I'm in enemy territory. I need a drink more than anyone here." He gave me a dramatic eye roll and flipped his hair back from his eyes. All it did was make him look even more adorable, especially since he was still wearing my jacket. I had to fight the urge to lean over and kiss him.

I ordered our drinks and asked the bartender if I could get word to Sam that I was here. Maybe give him a note or something. A waitress picking up drinks from the bar said she was heading toward the stage area. She would tell Sam I was there in the audience. I gave her my name and thanked her. I played in the same kinds of bars Sam did. Sometimes we played together. We always let each other know when we were at a show. It was good to know you were playing to at least one friendly face. Helped steady the nerves, I thought.

We were still at the bar when she came back to us and instructed us to follow her. We made our way to a very small table placed to the right of the makeshift stage.

"Sam reserved this table for guests. It's yours tonight." She gave me a flirtatious smile and seemed to flash a bit of cleavage as she leaned forward to place our drinks on the table.

Aaron noticed too. He gave her a cool smile and leaned back in his chair. He then sprung suddenly to his feet and shrugged off my jacket, making a big production of handing it back to me.

"Too hot for me now, Matty. Do you mind taking your jacket back for me?" He batted his eyelashes at me. Seriously. I noticed his voice had a more feminine note as well. Was he jealous of the waitress's attention? This was new territory for me. Once again, I felt unsure. The glass of vodka soda I ordered would help a little with my unease.

Aaron was uncharacteristically quiet for a few minutes once he took his seat again. He swept his gaze warily over the crowd as though trying to gage what sort of folks came to bars like this. I could tell he was feeling a little uncomfortable. He caught me watching him and flashed me one of his beautiful smiles before taking a big gulp of his vodka cranberry. I wasn't surprised when he started choking.

"Easy, big guy. There's no hurry." I patted him on the back the way my mom had always done to me when I was little. I'm not sure what she thought that would do, but that silly pat was an ingrained gesture in my family.

Aaron gave me a weak laugh as he regained composure.

"The bartender must have heard me ask for a stiff one. Ha! Pun only sort of intended." He laughed out loud at his own joke, and I couldn't help but join in. His laughter was infectious. "Better be careful, Matty. I get a little slutty when I've had too much. I don't want to do anything you'll regret in the morning." He giggled softly. Geez, I was beginning to wonder if Aaron had eaten at all. I leaned forward to ask him when the lights over the stage area went dark, announcing the evening's entertainment.

"Oooh, is this your friend? Sam, right? What does he sing anyway?" I was surprised I could hear Aaron's voice over the wolf whistles and cheering.

I smiled at him and just whispered in his ear, "You'll see." My lips gently brushed the tip of his ear. He started at my touch, but just turned forward in his seat to focus on Sam.

Sam Thompson and I had met in a criminal justice class my first year of law school. We were in the same study group and quickly learned that we shared a second passion in music. Sam was a year ahead of me in school and had been making a name for himself in the small club and bar scene, playing acoustic guitar and singing. He said it worked as a great stress reliever for him and gave him a life outside of textbooks and lectures. I'd been playing guitar since I was in my midteens. I was even in a small band in college. Like Sam, it was never my intention to make a living playing, but I loved it too.

Sam walked out with his six-string guitar draped over his shoulder. He made eye contact with me and gave me a nod before he sat on a small stool and adjusted the microphone in front of him. Sam looked the part of a soulful blues guitarist. His sandy-blond hair was a little long and shaggy. He had a lean and lanky build and was probably a good couple inches taller than me. He was dressed casually tonight in a worn pair of jeans and an ancient concert T-shirt. Sam was all about the music, not fashion.

I snuck a peek at my companion as I realized that, although I didn't know Aaron well at all, my guess would be that he liked to dress for whatever the occasion called. I hoped he wasn't going to hate being here tonight. Inviting him here was pure impulse on my part. I had no clue what I was doing. Once again. But Aaron seemed to bring out a carefree, go-with-the-flow side of me. If I thought too much about any of this, I knew I'd be in trouble. He was looking attentively toward the stage as Sam welcomed everyone and began to run his fingers over the strings of his guitar. I figured that as long as Aaron didn't expect him to play Lady Gaga, this could be all right.

Sam played for a good forty-five minutes to an enthusiastic audience before he announced he was taking a small break. During the set, I'd kept an eye on my companion while Sam played. I noticed Aaron would alternate his attention between Sam and the people gathered to listen to him. He reminded me of a wild, beautiful creature who somehow found himself in enemy territory. He looked wary and on guard but interested at the same time.

I leaned forward to ask him if wanted to head out when Sam approached our table. I stood to greet him and gave him a one-armed guy hug. Sam was on a performer's high, keyed up from the adrenaline rush playing in front of a crowd gives you when the nerves give way to the simple joy of playing the music you love. Sam and I both performed covers of music we liked. Mostly classic rock, but I also loved good pop music and would play anything from the Beatles to Maroon 5. I didn't think Aaron's taste in music ran in either direction, but so far, he seemed at least mildly entertained.

I introduced Aaron to Sam as Sam pulled up a chair to join us.

"You were awesome, man," I enthused, giving him a high five. "Let me buy you a drink."

"Thanks, but I'm good. I have so much work to do this weekend. I'm not drinking anything tonight."

Sam gave Aaron a brief once-over before asking him if we knew each other from law school. I don't know why that struck me as funny, but I gave a quick chuckle at the thought of Aaron in one of my boring classes. He was much too vibrant for Constitutional Law. I would have remembered someone like him. Aaron raised an eyebrow at me. I smiled at him, hoping to convey that I meant no insult.

"No, we met at a club and then a bar and now another bar. Creatures of the night, right, Matty?" Uh-oh. Aaron was on the defense now, and Sam was giving me the weirdest look. It was time to retreat.

"Right. Hey, Sam. We're gonna be heading out. Let me know when your next gig is, 'kay?" I started to get up from the table, but Sam grabbed my wrist before I got anywhere.

"Wait. I was going to ask you if you would come play a song or two with me. Come on, dude, it would be great. We can do a couple of the ones we practiced last week."

"Do it, Matty. I want to hear you." Aaron was the one giving funny looks now.

"Yeah, Matty…," Sam pleaded, drawing out my name to let me know he wanted to know when I'd gone from Matt to Matty.

"Alright, but only one, Sam. We haven't practiced enough. It's going to be edgy anyway. I'm assuming you have more than one guitar?" I figured it was easier to give in and then get out of here. I felt like I was paying for my impulsiveness now, and I really wanted out.

Sam slapped me hard on the back once and held out a hand to Aaron.

"Nice meeting you, Aaron. I'll introduce you right away so you can head out if you want afterwards. I appreciate it!"

"Shit!" I sighed. "I'm sorry, Aaron. You are probably so ready to get out of here. I'll just do the one song and we can go. Is that cool?"

"Matt. I want to hear you play. I'm totally cool. I'm not sure you realize this, but I'm here of my own free will. I know how to get a taxi home, and this isn't a date anyway, right?" I nodded in agreement. "Good. Because if it were you would have fed me before you started giving me this gut-rot vodka. I am going to have a headache in the morning for sure."

I ended up playing and singing three songs with Sam. I was having too much fun to quit after one, and Aaron looked like he was enjoying our impromptu concert anyway. The audience ate it up, just as Sam had predicted. We were definitely a little rusty since we hadn't practiced together in a while, but no one seemed to notice.

I gave Aaron a signal to follow me as I made my way toward the exit, giving my new fans high fives on my way outside. Aaron had grabbed my leather jacket and handed it to me once we were out in the cool evening air.

"You were really great. I think I recognized one song, but it was all terrific. You have a sweet, sexy voice, Matty. I like."

Aaron's compliment made me feel ten feet tall. I felt that adrenaline rush sweep over me and turn into fire deep inside. I was unbelievably horny, and although I knew exactly what I wanted, I had a feeling I wasn't going to get it tonight. I didn't want to take him home yet, regardless.

"Let me feed you. We need to counteract the bad vodka with a greasy burger or something. Sound good?"

I was rewarded with his beautiful smile.

Aaron pointed me toward a diner near his place that served all night. We ordered a huge plate of chili cheese fries to share and a pitcher of ice water.

"I love these fries, but I'm on a green diet starting tomorrow. Or I mean when I wake up. I can't believe how late it is. Way past my bedtime! I figured I'd go to my tame little work party, exit before I had the chance to embarrass myself in front of my coworkers, and then hang out with Jay for a while until Peter got home. Who knew I'd be swept away to a hetero bar to listen to top-forty music performed live and in concert in part by none other than the guy who whisked me away? A first for me." Aaron raised a chili fry in salute. There was a wicked gleam in his eye, so I knew he actually had enjoyed himself. I was suddenly very happy I'd gone with instinct this evening. It had been a lot of fun.

"Jay is your friend? Peter too?" We didn't know much about one another, but he'd met a few of my friends already, well, in passing anyway, and I didn't know anything about his.

"Mmm-hmm. Jay is my best friend, and Peter is his partner. In the land of gay, they are what I would wish for one day. They've been together almost five years and they just get each other. Peter is a very successful lobbyist, and he's super busy during election season, so I get to spend more time with Jay now than I usually would. I mean, we go to the gym and get coffee and that sort of thing all the time, but evenings are usually couple time or third-wheel time. Which I am all too familiar with."

I wanted to steer the conversation away from couple anything, so I asked Aaron about his other friends and other hobbies.

"Well, I run."

"Run? Like jog or do marathons? What do you mean?" I prompted. I couldn't help noticing that he definitely had a runner's lean physique.

"Yes to all. I do a lot of half marathons and 10Ks because I don't have the time to train for a full marathon. But my goal is to do the New York marathon next year and maybe qualify for the Boston the following year. Jay and most of my other friends that run are more into social running. Jay talks the whole time he runs and he tops out at three miles. You can't get any serious training done with that kind of ethic, but it's a great way to spend time with your friends if they're willing, so how can I complain?" He stopped to take a big gulp from his water glass.

"So, rain or shine? Or gym on days you don't run?"

"Every day or at least six days a week. I go to the gym for light weight lifting, and let's be honest, to check out the eye candy." He wiggled his eyebrows and looked positively adorable. It was all I could do not to touch him somehow. "Do you run?"

"Well, once in a while. I actually did a couple of miles last week, but mostly I work out at the gym and play a pickup game with friends on weekends when I can."

"Pickup game?"

"Yeah, basketball usually, but sometimes baseball or football too."

"Those sound a little dangerous, Matty. That's why I like running. Put your favorite tunes on, get your running shoes, and just go. And go."

"So you'd rather not talk for three miles, although how your friend can talk and run for that long shows some insane stamina if you ask me, right?"

"Ha! Yeah, Jay's got stamina. Well, I guess we'd have to ask Peter about that. I love running with friends, but I admit that I get in a zone when I run alone, and I can go for long stretches. Miles really."

"How many? I mean, what's the farthest you've ever gone before?"

Aaron wiggled his eyebrows suggestively again. He had a silly expression, which I think was meant to be lascivious, on his beautiful face. Instead, it was just fucking cute.

"What are you really asking me, Matty?" he teased. I gave him my best blank stare in response. Aaron sighed theatrically and took another long drink of water before answering me.

"Once I had just come home from visiting my family after some holiday or other and I just… I don't know, they're great, don't get me wrong. But they stress me out sometimes. I must have run sixteen miles when I got home. I didn't clue in until it got dark. See, it's a little like therapy."

"Yeah, I can see that. Everyone has their way, I guess."

"Sex would always be my first choice, but since it isn't always an option, I run." Aaron fluttered his eyelashes at me. He was flirting shamelessly, but I got the message it was to steer away from any chat about family. Sex talk as a diversion. Interesting, but also distracting.

By the time I took him back to his place, it was 3:00 a.m. The usually busy streets were virtually empty. A fine layer of fog from the river painted the low-lying shrubs and sidewalks in front of his building. It looked a little mystic and magical, as though the early morning hour still held promise. I pulled close to the curb, set the car in park, and turned toward my companion. I didn't want to say good-bye, yet I didn't know where this thing between us could go. I felt that familiar wave of frustration.

"Can I walk you up? I mean it. I just want to be sure you're safe." It sounded like a lame request, but Aaron seemed pleasantly surprised.

"You are a gentleman, aren't you?" His eyes twinkled. "I won't say no, and I'll try to keep my hands to myself. There's a parking spot up there. Take it so you don't get a ticket."

I parked the car as instructed and met Aaron at the curb. His smile lit his entire face. God, he was beautiful. He took my arm when I reached his side. I didn't protest, though the gesture seemed overly familiar. It just felt amazing to have this beautiful creature at my side looking at me like I was some kind of hero for offering to walk him to his door.

There was a bright lantern light on above the old glass and iron front door. Aaron couldn't get the latch to catch, so I took the key from him and gave it a try.

"It sticks sometimes," he muttered under his breath.

It opened easily for me. I was beginning to think my levels of chivalry were being tested. The thought made me grin when I should have been annoyed.

"You're my hero!" he whispered loudly.

"Knock it off. Where is your place?"

"Uh-oh, Matty's getting mad. Watch out, kids." Aaron pointed to the elevator off to the right. The corridor was not as well lit as the front alcove had been. I was actually glad I was making sure he was safe. I was a little nervous myself. Which must have shown on my face, because Aaron laughed outright as the elevator doors opened.

"Relax, sweetie. This isn't the Bates Motel. It's just an old building. Supposedly historic, but really it just means the lighting is poor and the water pressure is worse. My apartment is cute, though. Come see. You're safe."

I rolled my eyes this time but gamely followed him.

His apartment was on the fifth floor. He led me down another long hallway and stopped in front of 5E.

"Home sweet home," he said with a flourish as he opened his door. "Come make sure there are no bogeymen and then I promise to let you go, Matty."

Aaron turned on a light and breezed through his small entry into a larger living room. As I followed him, I took in my surroundings. The apartment was small, with an open floor plan. A tiny galley kitchen was situated to the right, with a small pass-through to the living room, which was five steps away from a small breakfast table with two chairs. The furniture was sparse, but that was probably best in the small space. I could tell it was all good quality and that his taste ran to modern design. The walls were painted white on one side and dark gray on the other, with a huge picture window showcased in between. The sofa was a lighter shade of gray, pushed against the dark-gray wall and strewn with bright pillows in red, orange, and yellow. It looked like one of those hip knock offs of a classic modern design that appeared cooler than it was comfortable. There was a huge black-and-white photograph of the Brooklyn Bridge above the sofa and a sleek flat screen TV along the opposite wall. The flat screen had to rival the one in my own apartment. My roommates and I had all chipped in on the largest model we could afford for optimal sports viewing. I smiled at the memory of Aaron telling me about all the reality television programs he watched.

I could see into his bedroom from the living area, and although it was dark, I could see the bed was neatly made. Aaron's entire apartment was immaculate. And the juxtaposition of his modern tastes and the apartment's older features, like the high ceilings and a floor heater, made for a homey and comfortable space. It was nice, and it suited Aaron perfectly.

Aaron threw his keys in the egg-shaped bright-orange bowl on his small kitchen table and turned around with his arms outstretched.

"Well, it's tiny, but it's all mine. As long as I pay the rent, that is."

"It's really nice. Suits you." I felt awkward as I stuffed my hands back in the leather jacket Aaron had returned to me earlier.

"Thanks for walking me up. That was very gentlemanly of you. Is that a word? Whatever, it was sweet."

His smile was a little shy, and his bangs had fallen back into his eyes. This time I couldn't help myself. I reached out to move his hair away from his eyes. He looked up at me in surprise, and my breath caught. We stared at one another for a second more before our mouths met. The kiss was sweet. Just a good night kiss until he ran his tongue over my bottom lip. I moaned out loud and met his tongue with my own. And just as suddenly, the kiss turned urgent. I ran my fingers through his dark hair and cupped his neck with my other hand. I wanted him as close to me as possible. His lips were the perfect combination of soft and pliant. He moved his hands underneath my jacket and pulled my T-shirt out of my jeans. I felt his cool touch on the sensitive small of my back and shivered as he splayed his hands over my bare skin.

Our mouths were moving in a frenzy. I kissed and licked along his jawline, nibbled at his ear, and finally licked a path along the smooth skin of his neck. His cheek had the smallest trace of stubble. The light abrasion was intoxicating. I licked and sucked my way across his clavicle, unbuttoning his shirt to get to his skin. I heard him moan aloud. His hands caressed down my sides and made their way to my crotch. He lightly cupped me through my jeans and then took a firmer hold, as if waiting for my reaction. I held my breath as he unbuckled my belt, unzipped my jeans, and wrapped his long fingers around my shaft. My lips were at his throat, and I bit him lightly as he moved his palm up and down over my boxer-briefs. I cupped his ass, grinding our bodies close with his hand caught in between. He pushed me back an inch to gently move his hand inside the elastic of my briefs.

His bare hand on my naked cock was nearly my undoing. I was rock hard and desperate for friction. I reached out to bring him close again, but he resisted. I opened my eyes, not realizing I'd closed them in the heat of passion. He looked up at me, his lust-filled eyes half-closed, and kissed me once more with his tongue before he sank to his knees in front of me.

I could barely catch my breath, let alone think straight, and I felt perilously close to fainting when he kissed the head of my dick. It was just a touch of lips to that most sensitive skin. Just a tease. He pushed my jeans further down my shaky legs and kneaded the muscles of my ass as he opened his mouth to swallow my entire length. I squeezed my eyes shut, trying to concentrate on not coming, but I had to see him. He looked up at me, licked at the precum dripping from my slit, and moved one of his hands around to fondle my balls. He ran his tongue over one ball and then the other before returning to suck wildly on my cock. I could see his head bobbing up and down and feel the sweet, wet suction of his luscious mouth. I ran my hands through his hair, encouraging his motion, but I knew I was in danger of coming soon. I could feel that familiar tingle at the base of my balls and knew I had to warn him I was about to shoot.

"Aar, Aaron... I'm gonna. You need to stop." My voice sounded so strangled, I wondered if he heard me.

And then I came. I shook with the force of it and held onto his shoulders for support. He swallowed and swallowed, then licked. His eyes were closed but his expression was a gorgeous mixture of lust and bliss. When he looked up and opened his beautiful hazel eyes, he gave me that amazing smile.

I laughed. It was sheer beauty. The perfect melding of all the senses. I wanted to thank him, but really, I wasn't sure what I was supposed to do now. Return the favor? I'd never sucked a guy off before. I would do it, though, if Aaron wanted me to. At that very moment, I would have done anything Aaron wanted.

He got back to his feet and looked up at me. He kissed me gently, but I needed more than a chaste peck. I licked at his mouth until he opened up for me, and I tasted myself on his tongue. It was exhilarating. I couldn't believe what had just happened here.

"Good night, Matty." I opened my eyes quickly as Aaron broke the kiss and stepped away from me.

"Don't you want me to...." I know I was blushing. I couldn't even say the words out loud. I could feel the high from the most amazing orgasm I'd ever experienced crash around me, leaving me feeling more unsure and awkward than I'd felt in a years.

"No, you don't have to... but thank you." He moved toward his door and opened it as I struggled to get myself back together.

"Are you okay? Did I do… or not do something I should have?" I was stumbling and probably making a total ass of myself, but I had to know where we stood. I didn't know him very well, but the desire to change that was instinctual. The problem was I needed his guidance. I was in over my head.

"Don't be silly. You're fabulous. And sexy as hell. But it is three, probably later now, in the morning and…."

"Yeah, sorry. You're right. I'll go now. Can I… can I call you?" I probably sounded desperate but wasn't sure how to play it cool now.

"Sure. Yes. See you, Matty." Aaron's expression was guarded now. It was time to retreat, and he was right, it was really late. I'm sure I was no longer thinking clearly anyway.

I bent down and gently kissed him on the lips, then once again on his forehead before I turned and walked to the elevator. I looked back at his door once more while I waited and saw him leaning on the doorframe, watching me. He gave me a small wave and a tired smile before closing the door.

I kept my head as clear as possible as I rode the elevator down. The cool early morning air helped me keep calm. I reached my car, climbed inside, and felt the wall begin to crumble. I began to shake. I struggled to get myself under control, thinking at first it was just the cold from outside that had me shaking. The tears were harder to explain. What was I doing? I was a grown man sitting in my car crying after experiencing the most intense blow job ever. Oh, yeah… given by a man. I knew I had more to deal with now than cheating on my girlfriend. I needed to figure out who I was, what I wanted. Because I couldn't deny I wanted Aaron.

| 3 |

IN THE weeks that followed, I thought of Aaron constantly. I didn't contact him again. I knew I was the one with issues. He was kind enough to put it mildly, but I understood the ball was in my court. To say I was confused didn't scratch the surface.

I was ridiculously busy with school projects and working at the law firm. I knew I was using school and work as a means of escape. I was putting off dealing with something I knew wasn't going away anytime soon. I spoke to Kristin a few times on the phone, and our conversations were polite but stilted. I had a feeling she knew something was up. Heck, maybe she was trying to figure out how to break up with me. The problem for me wasn't only that I realized I needed out of my relationship with Kristin. It was more about trying to figure out what I wanted after that. Aaron hadn't called me, which should clue me in to the fact that maybe he wasn't as interested in me as I was in him. It was all a little pathetic.

Thanksgiving was around the corner, and for the first time since I had left for college, I was really looking forward to going home. I was looking forward to the things I knew I could count on, like my mother's cooking, watching football with my dad and my brother, listening to my teenage twin sisters bicker about chores and clothes swapping, and our old lab panting at my feet, begging for scraps of food at the dinner table. I craved something I could be sure of since I certainly wasn't feeling sure of myself.

I was from a small town outside of Pittsburgh. I didn't go home often anymore. School and now my internship kept me tied to the city. So when I did visit, it usually worked out that I was really excited to see everyone for the first couple of days, on my way to annoyed the third day, and really ready to get back to DC by day four. I guess that is family for you.

It was no different this visit, with one exception. Me. I participated in all the family traditions. I played a game of touch football with our extended family on Thanksgiving morning, helped dad bring chairs and tables out of storage for the traditional feast, roughhoused with my brother, and teased my older sister and the twins. But I noticed my mom watching me a little more closely than usual. She asked, as she always did, about whom I was dating, about Kristin. She was curious about when she had gone home to visit her family in New York and what sorts of things we'd been up to recently. Innocent stuff, like what movies or restaurants had we been to. But she must have read something in my responses, because she didn't delve as deep as usual, and I noticed her watchful eye on me during my entire stay. She was worried about me, and what could I say… I was worried about me too.

On my last morning at home, I decided to go for an early run. There had been a light snow the night before, leaving our quiet tree-lined residential street with a whisper of white on every surface. As I had told Aaron, I didn't run often, but I was looking forward to it this morning. Almost as if, by participating in something he enjoyed doing, I could be close to him. Crazy, I know.

I was doing a few last-minute stretches before taking off when I heard my brother, Sean, call after me.

"Wait up!" He bounded down the front steps of our parents' two-story colonial, slamming the door behind him. I'm sure our parents loved that.

"Hey, I saw you about to take off. I'm going for a run too, so we may as well go together." Sean gave me a devilish smile. The kind of smile that usually meant trouble, although I didn't see what harm him joining me would do. Besides, unlike Aaron, I don't talk much when I run, and the company was nice.

Well, maybe not. Sean wanted to talk. And he wasn't really capable of running and talking, which meant he was panting and running or we were jogging really slowly. Not what I had in mind.

Sean is older than me by a year. He's technically my stepbrother. My mom married his dad when I was five and my sister, Shelly, was seven. Our twin sisters, Sarah and Samantha, were born a couple years later. Sean and I have always been tight. He was the one who always got into trouble, and I was usually stupid enough to follow. He'd always possessed boundless energy and enthusiasm. Sean was an avid outdoorsman, and like myself, a lover of all sports. He was one of those people who was constantly in motion and always talking. The only thing was, he wasn't much of a runner.

As we slowly started down our street, it started. He chattered about everything from the weather (cold as a witch's tit) to our cousin Jessica's baby announcement during Thanksgiving dinner (awkward, and will she ever marry that bum?) to how the Steelers should crush it again this year. Mostly I listened. Sean didn't usually require response. He just liked an audience. Which was why I missed his question until he literally stopped midrun in exasperation. I turned back, jogging in place, and asked what was up.

"I asked you a question, moron. What is up with you? You're being weird."

I sighed and inclined my head, indicating I would talk if he would run. He gave an even bigger sigh and jogged to catch up.

"I'm probably going to break things off with Kristin." It was really the only safe explanation I had for my distractedness. I should have known he wouldn't buy it.

"So? Come on, man. It's pretty obvious that she isn't the one. Don't tell me she's breaking out the wedding magazines?"

"Well, not exactly. But there's been wedding talk because some friends are tying the knot. It's not that, though. I just… I don't know. I feel like I'm being unfair to her. I'm not that into it, and I guess I just need to make a clean break." I paused for a couple minutes, during which Sean was remarkably silent. "I forgot to call her on Thanksgiving. I actually didn't think about it until the next day, and I felt terrible. When I did call she was a little hurt but was understanding. She said she got that I was busy with all the family over, yada yada…. And that's another thing, I guess. She never gets angry and doesn't really have any expectations of me. Which, yeah, that's great… except I get the feeling you're supposed to have those expectations about someone you care about. Like you'd be mortally offended if your significant other didn't respect you enough to think of you on a major holiday."

I wasn't going to mention who I did think of all day. I actually had sent him a text too. My first attempt at communication in a couple weeks. He returned the simple "Happy Thanksgiving" from me with a smile face emoticon and "Happy Turkey Day, Matty." It was funny how that silly exchange had me smiling for the rest of the day. I was able to forget for a while that I needed to deal with Kristin when I got back to DC, and deal with myself. Was I bi? Probably. Or just gay for Aaron? And even if I acknowledged the bi part, to myself at least, was I ready to pursue a relationship with a man? No one who knew me had the slightest idea I was attracted to men. This would be more involved than I was able to comprehend at the moment.

"Wow. You really are an asshole." Sean shook me out of my inner reverie. "You don't call her on Thanksgiving and then don't like that she wasn't really pissed at you when you finally remember her the next fucking day. I thought I was the one with the heartbreaker rep. Turns out it's Saint Matthew breaking the girls' hearts."

"Fuck off. I'm just trying to tell you that I acknowledge I was a dick. I'm not who I want to be or who I should be with Kristin. We both deserve something or someone else. Maybe I just need to concentrate on finishing my degree and working at the law firm right now. Relationships are too taxing. Ya know?"

Sean gave me an appraising look, though to his credit, he didn't stop jogging.

"You're full of shit. I'm your brother. I know you. Who is she? I know there's someone else. I saw your face on Thanksgiving when you got that text message." I gave him an incredulous look. "What? I can put two and two together. Lower the sound on your ringer, man. Basically you advertised that you were getting a text, you read it, and then got all moony. You went from being all quiet and moody to life of the party…. Slight exaggeration, maybe, but I know you. Something else is going on too." He looked at me, expecting some big explanation. He rolled his eyes at me when he realized I wasn't sharing.

"Hey, Matt? Seriously, though. Just be happy. Kristin is a nice girl, but you're right. You need something different. If your secret texter is what you need, go for it. You deserve to be happy." This was a surprise. I didn't say anything right away as I half-wondered what Sean would say if he knew who my "secret texter" was.

"So, if you're done with her, can I give her a call?" Okay, so maybe I wasn't surprised. "I'll wait an appropriate amount of time. What should it be? Maybe a week or two?" He ruined his request with the stupid grin, letting me know he was after my reaction and not my soon-to-be ex-girlfriend.

"Now who's the asshole?" I picked up my pace, but Sean kept up with me.

"You're a prick."

"I know you are but what am I?" And on it went.

We were both sweaty and gross when we finally got back to the house. Sean wanted to challenge me to a game of horse at the old basketball hoop in our driveway. It was a game we'd played together for the nineteen years we'd been saddled with each other through our parents' marriage. It was a great way to restore my equilibrium. I was suddenly very thankful for my family. Somehow I felt a little more prepared to deal with the real world.

DEALING with the real world was overrated. I was slammed with memos and papers to write at school. Finals were around the corner. Plus there was a big case one of the lawyers at the firm was working on and I was given the daunting task of research, which meant hours poring through law journals. It was easy to stay in full denial with my current workload. I dodged calls from Kristin and made a point of returning her calls when I knew she was in class. My brother was right... I was an asshole. It was eating me up, though. I knew I would have to talk to Kristin. Avoidance would only work for so long.

The following Friday morning, my cell rang very loudly at an ungodly hour. Sean was right, I needed to turn the ringer down. Because I was startled out of sleep, I didn't check to see who the caller was. It was Kristin. I was groggy with sleep, and I struggled to figure out what my approach should be. I hadn't formulated a plan, and 6:00 a.m. on any given day wasn't the best time to begin. As luck would have it, I got another reprieve. She was calling to remind me that she would be at a bachelorette party that weekend but was really hoping we could grab a bite to eat or something Sunday night. Of course I agreed. That gave me a two-day reprieve. Until she dropped the other reminder.

I'd really only been half-listening but tuned in when she repeated her questions.

"You remember the wedding is next weekend, right? Matt? Hello?"

"Uh, yeah. Next Saturday. Got it." Smooth one, Matt. Now what do I do? End this Sunday or wait until after her friend's wedding, which I'd promised I'd go to months ago, to break up? I couldn't seem to win here.

"Did you get your tux cleaned? I can take it for you if you want. I know you've been so busy lately." She paused when I didn't answer. "I really miss you, Matt. It feels like forever since we've been able to spend any time together."

Kristin's voice was almost a whisper. She sounded sad. And worse yet, she sounded 100 percent sincere. Fuck.

"I know. Dinner Sunday sounds good." That was the best I could manage. When she agreed and we set a time for me to pick her up, I noticed she once again didn't seem bothered by any lack of real emotion from me.

I turned off my phone for the rest of the day and concentrated on writing my papers for school. I had a pretty decent night's sleep and woke up feeling refreshed. I was also dying for some outdoor exercise. I thought of Aaron, as I did many times during any given day lately, as I laced up my running shoes. Where did he run? Maybe I'd see him? I purposefully hadn't called or sent him a text since Thanksgiving. I wouldn't let myself until I'd broken up with Kristin.

MONTROSE PARK was one of Georgetown's best-kept secrets. It was part of the much larger Rock Creek Park, but it was not nearly as well known, which meant it was a great place for a quiet run relatively close by. In early December, most of the leaves had long since fallen. It was like a scenic wonderland in the middle of the nation's capital. I hadn't run in the park in a while, and I found myself looking forward to the peaceful atmosphere.

I had a full day of writing ahead of me, so I knew my run couldn't be too long. I put my ear buds in, turned my music on, and jogged up Thirty-First Street toward the park. It felt invigorating and relaxing at the same time. I had decided I needed to do this more often when I noticed a familiar form jogging out of the Montrose Park main entry. I was fairly certain it was Aaron. He was with another man. Maybe his friend Jay? I didn't think so, though. This guy looked older than Aaron by at least ten years. He was definitely fit, but he was shaved bald and had a Mr. Clean muscular physique. Was Aaron seeing this guy? He said he didn't have a boyfriend, but of course that didn't mean he didn't go out with other men. Or maybe they'd just met and were a new item.

Aaron was dressed in tight black running pants and a black pullover with neon-green trim. His running shoes matched his jacket, which made me smile. He looked good. He didn't seem winded at all, but his running partner looked a little sweaty. They had probably just finished a run in the park, and I guessed they were heading back toward the bridge.

I was overcome with curiosity. I kept my pace but adjusted my path to follow Aaron and his friend as discreetly as possible. If he saw me, I would feign surprise. Geez, now I was stalking. Was there no end to my idiocy?

They kept a steady pace down R Street toward the river, but then turned right onto Cambridge Place. I really couldn't follow down this street without them noticing. It was a quiet residential street and it was still early morning. I would definitely be in more danger of Aaron noticing me. Plus feigning surprise at running into him most likely wouldn't be believable. I was about to retrace my path back toward the park, as I had originally intended, when Aaron's running partner stopped suddenly and Aaron came to a halt beside him. The older man gave a quick glance up and down the mostly deserted street before wrapping his hand around Aaron's neck and drawing him in for a quick but passionate kiss. Aaron smiled when the man pulled away, then turned to jog up the street, leaving his partner to follow him.

I felt sick to my stomach, like I'd been punched straight on with no warning and no protection. Ridiculous, I know. I had no claims to Aaron whatsoever. If anything, I was just a creepy stalking voyeur. Chastising myself didn't help me regain my calm, however. Truthfully, I felt betrayed too. Unreasonable, I know that, but I realized then and there, as I pushed myself running much faster than my normal pace, that I wanted him. I didn't want to share him either. Since when does anyone get what he wants without working for it? I needed to figure out a plan.

Simply put, I wanted Aaron. This would suggest I was a bisexual man and not the heterosexual one my family, friends, and even acquaintances knew me to be. Whether or not Aaron would be interested in something more with me was still an unknown, but I could no longer deny that this feeling wasn't going away anytime soon. My reaction to seeing him with another guy told me this loud and clear.

Back at home I could barely concentrate on writing the paper, and I'd used my workload to beg off from hanging out with my friends. They could tell something was up with me, but they left me alone. Each one of us had gone through the staggering stress of law school, work, and relationship bullshit. They probably sensed, correctly, that it was my turn. When I found myself in complete textbook overload, I picked up my guitar. Playing always calmed my nerves.

By the next day, I had gained a little perspective. I knew the first thing I had to do was be honest with Kristin and break things off. If she wanted me to go to the wedding still, I would. I had always considered Kristin a friend, and if possible, I wanted us to remain so. The next step was for me to concentrate on finals, work, and getting through the holidays. I wouldn't try to contact Aaron until my finals were complete, thinking I could use the extra time to work out how I could approach him without sounding weird or desperate. This was new territory for me. For the first time ever, I wanted to pursue a man romantically.

I arrived to pick up Kristin at her place later that night for dinner. She opened her door wearing a giant smile and little else. I audibly gulped, I'm sure. She probably figured my reaction to be the opposite of what it truly was. Fuck. This was not going to be easy.

"Hi, gorgeous," she purred. Not kidding, she sounded like a sex kitten. This was not Kristin. Nor was the getup. She was wearing a one-piece sexy black lacy number that pushed up her small breasts, giving them a rounded effect at the top. She had never once worn lingerie in the year we'd been dating. Something was up. The funny thing was that it wasn't my cock. If I was having any second thoughts, seeing the usually conservative Kristin in a skimpy getup should have gotten the blood pumping. Instead, I was painfully uncomfortable with how I could now see the direction this evening was headed. Especially once I got a view of the table carefully set for two behind her, laid with her grandmother's crystal wine glasses and china. Soft jazz music was playing from her speakers, setting a scene for seduction. Crap.

"Uh, wow, um, what's all this?" I asked lamely as she flung herself at me, wrapping her small body around me. Her long honey-blonde hair was in my face, and I could smell the body oils and perfumes she must have recently applied.

"I've missed you, silly goose. Matt, we haven't seen each other in forever. I really, really missed you." The way she was grinding her body on me left no mistaking what she missed. I gently pulled out of her grasp and walked toward the table set with candlelight and roses. My head was pounding, and I was about as far from hungry as a guy could be without hanging over a porcelain bowl.

"Um, didn't you want to go out for dinner?" My voice was weak and it was possible she didn't even hear me.

"Well," she said, coming to stand beside me at the table. She sounded a little cooler this time, maybe cluing in to my tepid response. "My roommates are out, and I thought we could take advantage of having the place to ourselves tonight." She turned on a huskier-sounding tone than I was used to hearing from her. "We can play and then have dinner later. I'll even serve you dinner in bed if you get hungry for food."

I couldn't speak or move. And when an uncomfortable minute of silence passed, she backed away from me and went into her bedroom. Shit, did she expect me to follow? I really didn't think so. I knew that I could forget the whole thing by following her into her room and taking advantage of what she was so blatantly offering. Instead, I let the moment pass and gave her a weak smile when she came out covered in an old terrycloth bathrobe. She didn't return the smile.

"What's going on, Matt?" she asked coolly. She took a seat on the white slipcovered sofa, curling her legs underneath her body and hugging one of her bright floral pillows to her chest.

I took a deep breath. And then another to see if it would help, but it didn't. I moved toward her and perched myself on the armchair across from her, still unable to look at her. I hated hurting her. I wished I could love her so none of this was necessary. But I didn't love her. It wasn't fair to keep up even a casual dating thing with her when my thoughts were constantly with someone else. Pretending everything was cool wasn't working.

"I'm sorry."

Kristin gasped. I looked up at her finally. Her eyes were huge and wet with unshed tears. I felt about two feet tall.

I tried again. "I'm sorry, Kristin. I can't... I'm not.... Look, it's not...."

"Are you really going to say it's not you, it's me? Oh my God. I can't believe what a fucking idiot I am. I'm so embarrassed. Look at me. Just go... please, Matt. Please." She was crying in earnest now.

Instinctively I went to her side. She let me hold her for a couple seconds before pushing me away.

"Did you meet someone else? Is that it? Or is it the wedding? You don't have to go with me." Her anger was quickly taking a strange turn, and I knew I needed to say what I had to say and retreat. I couldn't make this right any other way. I was hurting someone I cared about, and it just couldn't be helped.

"Kristin, as lame as it sounds, it isn't you, it is me. I'm sorry. You deserve something I'm not. I really care for you. You are amazing. But honestly, I mean, look at the last few months... I'm way too wound up with school and work. I just can't be a good boyfriend to you. I can't do this. I don't want to hurt you. I want us to be friends, if you're okay with it. But I don't... I don't want the couple part." I was rambling, but she was listening, which I took as a positive sign. "I am sorry."

The silence was heavy, like wearing a winter coat in July.

"Can you go, please? I just need you to leave." Tears were running down her face. I wanted to help, but I'd caused this. She was right, I should leave.

I stood up slowly and let myself out. I wondered if I'd feel lighter now that it was done. I didn't. The guilt was crushing.

I made my way back to my apartment to find Curt on the sofa with a giant bowl of popcorn. The living room was dark, and an old black-and-white movie was on the big screen television.

"Oh, hi. I thought you were with Kristin tonight. I'm having 'classic cinema night, party of one'"—Curt actually did use his air quotes—"or two. Wanna watch?"

I didn't answer right away. I didn't know what to do now. I guess beer, popcorn, and an old movie sounded okay.

"Sure. Sounds good. Wanna beer?"

"No. I'm not drinking a drop tonight. I am literally buried in work. My concentration was off so I decided to go mindless for the rest of the night. What happened with you? Did she take one look at your ugly shirt and send you home?" When I remained silent, Curt turned to look at me more closely. "Hey, you okay?"

Curt had become one of my closest friends since I'd moved to DC two years ago. He was funny in a self-deprecating way, quick-witted, super intelligent, and fiercely protective of those he cared about. I'd known he was gay all along. He wasn't overtly gay in any way. He didn't advertise, but he had been up front with all of us from the start. His mantra was "be honest about who you are and good things will come." I knew he'd been out since his freshman year of college. Curt never spoke much about his relationship with his family, but he had tons of friends, gay and straight. His generosity of spirit drew people to him. I was grateful to be counted amongst his friends.

After the catastrophe I'd made of breaking up with Kristin, Curt's company was appreciated.

"Did something happen with you and Kri—"

"We broke up," I interrupted. I may as well get used to saying it. Everyone would be asking what happened.

Curt didn't say a word. He pushed the popcorn bowl toward me, put his feet up on the coffee table, and turned the volume up on the movie.

"Aren't you going to ask me about it?"

Curt paused the movie and turned to me. "Okay. What happened?"

I let out a long, tired sigh. "I just couldn't do it anymore, ya know? Have you ever been with someone where you know you don't want the same things? I started to dread her phone calls, and I just—"

Curt stopped me with a raised hand. "Matt. You don't have to defend yourself. Sometimes when it's over, it's over. It's not like you were married to her and you didn't leave her for someone else... did you?" His eyes took on a look of intense scrutiny.

"No. There isn't anyone else." I had a painful sudden memory of Aaron being kissed by his running partner. The jealousy felt fresh and raw. Curt must have noticed a change in my expression, but I cut him off. "Really. There was someone I was interested in, but I think I need to figure some things out first, and just like you, I'm buried in work and school. I need a clear head."

I don't know why, but I could hear Aaron's voice in my head saying, in that teasing lascivious voice he'd used the last night I was with him, "What you clearly need is head, honey." I laughed out loud.

Curt looked concerned, as though he was afraid I was unraveling in front of him. I sought to reassure him, because honestly, I finally felt a little lighter. I would get through finals and the holiday and then see if maybe, maybe I had a chance at all with Aaron.

| 4 |

I WENT home for the Christmas holidays as usual. It was a great visit. The burden of finals was over, and I had two weeks off before I returned to my internship. I told my family about my breakup with Kristin. No one seemed too surprised. My mom least of all.

"Honey, she wasn't right for you. You knew it. Just as you'll know when you do meet the right one." Of course she was right. The New Year suddenly seemed full of possibility.

January isn't one of my favorite months. It's cold and gloomy, and this year the weather was wicked. We got serious winters in Pittsburgh. This wasn't quite that dramatic, but nonetheless, roads were shut down regularly, flights cancelled, trains delayed. The snow seemed to fall every day. Not fun for the average guy trying to trudge to class through the messy white stuff. I was making my way toward campus one morning through the powdery snow that had fallen the night before. The morning was gloomy, but it wasn't supposed to snow again that day, so I had high hopes we'd actually see the sun.

My usual path was blocked by what looked like a photoshoot near the campus quad. I stopped short when I caught sight of

Aaron's familiar form. My heart started beating a rapid tattoo, and my face was flush with heat in spite of the bracing chill. I hadn't seen Aaron in over a month. Not since that day I'd seen him jogging with the man who'd kissed him. Our last communication of any kind was text messages sent on Thanksgiving. But I'd thought of him every day. I hadn't worked up the courage to contact him, even though I was completely free to do so now without guilt. Truthfully, what stopped me was my own coming to terms with my bisexuality and realizing it would take some courage. I couldn't deny my attraction to Aaron, though. Something about him was magnetic.

Aaron was dressed for the weather in a gorgeous long navy wool coat. He had a gray scarf around his neck and black weatherproof lace-up boots with fur lining. He wasn't wearing a hat, and his beautiful black hair was a bit longer than the last time I'd seen him. That familiar itch to run my fingers through it sent a tingle of sensation through my hand. He was holding a clipboard and chatting animatedly with a cute curly-haired girl dressed in one of those Michelin Man-like winter coats, with a hat pulled over her head and curls spilling out. She was giggling at something Aaron had said. Neither seemed to be paying much attention to the photographer and what looked, upon closer examination, to be a couple of models. Obviously it was a fashion shoot. There had to be a dozen or so people milling about the roped-off little area in the quad. Maybe Aaron and his friend were taking a break.

I overheard someone in the crew ask for a steamed latte. Aaron turned back toward the speaker, writing something on his clipboard as he turned to walk up the path.

"Aar, you want me to come with? I can help carry." That was the curly-haired girl.

"You mean you can help spill, klutz. I got it. Be back in a flash."

Aaron took a note from the clipboard and handed it back to his friend before walking toward the campus coffee shop up the hill.

"Aaron!" I called after him. I was a little flustered. I had no idea what to say now that he was here in front of me.

He looked at me curiously, and my heart sank when I realized he didn't recognize me.

"Sorry, it's been a while. Matt. Um, I guess we last texted at Thanksgiving." Lame. Ugh! My lack of cool around him shouldn't have surprised me by now, but this was ridiculous.

"Matty. Hi. I just didn't recognize you right away with all the winter gear." He flashed me that amazing smile, the one that made his hazel eyes twinkle, and I felt something settle inside me. I took my beanie off, figuring he'd recognize me better without it. "Yes, there you are! How've you been? Do you mind telling me about it while I walk to the coffee shop, though? I'm technically working while I get coffee for the crew."

Class was beginning in ten minutes for me. I'd be late for sure. I shrugged and followed Aaron. There really was no other choice.

"Sure. I'm good. How about you? I mean, how've you been? It's been a while." There I was again... Mr. Smooth.

"Hmm. Yeah, I remember." He didn't sound angry, more like teasing. Aaron was that strange personality we all run into once in a while that is overly familiar in ways that make you feel you're two steps behind. You want to catch up, but they always seem to know more about you than you do. Was he bringing up our night together two months ago as if it had been as earth-shattering for him as it was for me? More likely, I was reading too much into his friendliness. And Aaron was definitely friendly.

"So you're working with your favorite photographer?" I nodded back toward the fashion shoot now in the distance.

"You remember. Actually, no, Jean Paul isn't my favorite. He's a little unorganized for my taste. But no complaints here. It got me out of the office on a not-as-crappy-as-usual-weather day, and I've run into you again!"

I smiled at him. He was charming and full of life. But he was working, and I had to get to class, so as much as I wanted to continue our exchange, it couldn't be now. I wanted a chance to really talk to him.

"Yeah. Hey, I have to get to class and I know you have to work, but can I see you, Aaron?"

"Sure!" The answer came off too brightly. Maybe he was pissed after all. "Call me."

"Aaron." I couldn't blow this. He had to know I was serious. I really wanted a chance if he'd give me one. "I'm serious. I...."

"Look, Matt." He spoke in a soft and slow tone, as if trying to be as kind as possible. That sinking feeling was back in full force. "I don't think this is a good idea. I've been doing some thinking, making New Year's resolutions, etcetera. I can't get involved with someone who (a) has a girlfriend, wife, boyfriend or anyone other than me, period. Or (b) is buried in a closet. I'm not hiding for anyone. And if I remember correctly, because yes, it has been a while, you are both (a) attached and (b) not in tune with the side of you that kind of digs getting sucked off by a guy. You're a good guy, Matt. I'm glad we met, but that's all."

He looked me in the eye again, sighing heavily. "Bye, Matt. Take care of yourself." He turned away quickly and set a brisk pace with his head down.

"No, wait, Aaron." I jogged after him. "I don't have a girlfriend. I broke up with Kristin last month."

He stopped walking again and looked at me carefully with his head cocked to one side. I could see he was going to shut me down again, and I felt a desperate need to plead my case, smoothly or not.

"I know I'm a bit of a head case, but I don't have A and I'm willing to work on B. Just please... will you give me a chance?" Definitely desperate. I wondered if he knew I'd never made a plea like this for a girl. Ever.

"Matt. I can't. I'm sorry." I jumped in front of him before he could move away from me and grabbed onto his arm. He looked at my gloved hand on his coat and then at me, as if asking, "What the fuck, psycho?" I couldn't blame him, but I also couldn't stop trying.

"Friends. We can just be friends," I pleaded. And the look I received was nothing short of incredulous.

"Huh?" Good. I'd caught him off guard.

"You can't have too many friends, right? And friends can ask friends out for coffee or movies or even dinner. True?" Aaron nodded slowly, as if waiting for the punch line. "If that's all you can do right now, I'm cool with it."

I had his attention now, so I pressed a bit further.

"Aaron, if I'm totally honest here, there isn't a day that's gone by since I first met you at that fucking club that I haven't thought of you. I'm not totally baggage free, I get that, but I can't deny that I want you. Or whatever you'll give me. I just want a chance. And if it's friends… I would be honored to be your friend."

He stared at me openmouthed. I tucked my thumb under his chin to close it and gave him a smile I knew was more confident than I was feeling.

"What's the matter? You have too many friends?"

"Uh… no. Well, maybe." His composure had slipped, and it was adorable to see him trying to regain his footing. "Okay."

"Okay?"

"Yeah, we can be friends."

"So, just to clarify… that means if I wake up on a Saturday morning and want to grab a cup of coffee, I could call… say, my friend Aaron to join me and it wouldn't be weird? Or if I wanted to see a show I think Aaron would like, I could call him and invite him? Or…."

"Oh, for fuck's sake! Sure." His face was a little red, and it might have been from the cold, but I had a feeling I'd made him blush.

"Great! Well, then. I'll call you, Aaron. I promise." My smile felt like it was splitting my face in two. I took a chance and leaned in to give him a quick kiss on the cheek. I hurried away from him, intent now on getting to my class, but I couldn't resist looking back at him. He was still standing in the middle of the path, staring after me. The urge to let out a celebratory yell and throw my fist in the air in triumph was strong, but I held onto my cool, smiling widely all the way to class.

A COURSE of action was required here. I had Aaron's attention, but I didn't want to screw up by being overly smothering or by playing it too cool and not calling soon enough. Then I would be in danger of him thinking anything I'd said was bullshit. I had to figure out how to be his friend. I'd never pursued a friend before. Those things happened naturally, I'd always assumed. You had a common interest in sports, went to the same school, or even worked together. Aaron and I had none of that. I doubted he liked sports, in fact; trying to picture him watching football with my buddies made me laugh outright. I wasn't stereotyping. I mean, Curt was into football and baseball, and he loved a game of pickup basketball as much as the rest of my buddies. But Aaron wasn't anything like Curt. I guess I needed to find out for sure, but I would have bet money I was right about the sports.

Which left school or work as possible common ties, and we obviously had neither. I had a feeling music wasn't something we had in common either. I know he'd enjoyed that night at the bar with live music, but part of me knew he was humoring me. Dance music was his thing. Again, I'd bet on it.

I had to get to know Aaron as a friend with whom I didn't have anything obvious in common. Well, other than a hot kiss and sizzling blow job. Since those weren't on the table for now, I'd have to go about this the old-fashioned way. I'd have to ask questions and hope he'd agree to spend time with me. Platonically. Which hopefully would lead to something more. Eventually. I hoped.

I called him the day after I saw him on campus. I waited until early evening, thinking more than twenty-four hours was good. Another day might have been considered too much time. Yes, I realized I was in danger of over thinking. I just didn't want to fuck this up. I could end up being a lousy friend before I even got the chance to be a lousy boyfriend. Boyfriend. The thought made me smile. I took that as a good sign.

Aaron picked up his cell on the third ring, sounding a little winded.

"Hey."

"Hi, friend. It's Matt."

"Ha. Yes, I know. I still have your name in my phone." That sounded promising, I thought with a grin.

"How's it going? You sound out of breath. Did I catch you at a bad time?"

"No, I just finished a run. I'm walking home so now's a good time. Friend."

I smiled at his playful tone, but his mention of running made me think of the running partner I'd seen him kiss last month. A friend can ask about those things, right? I just had to be tactful and hope the blazing flash of jealousy I felt at the memory wouldn't surface and freak him out.

"You don't run alone, do you? I mean, it gets dark now early. It's not really safe."

"Tonight I ran alone. But I don't always. If I run alone, I stay on well-lit paths. Don't worry, friend. I'm not as big as you, but I'm still a big boy."

"I could run with you sometime. That's a good friend thing to do together, right?"

"Ha! A good friend thing? You did not just say that out loud. You are adorable! I mean that as a friend, of course. Yeah, I guess running together is a great friend activity."

"Great. When do you want to go?"

"Geez Louise. Um, how about Saturday morning? Early. You're in Georgetown, yeah? Give me your address and we can run near the campus. I know some decent routes out there. Sound good?"

"Yeah, sounds good." I gave him my information and was smiling when we hung up a minute later. I wanted to ask what he was doing tonight, what his week had been like, and what his plans were for Friday night. Three more days seemed like such a long time to wait. But I sensed the need to take this slowly if I wanted Aaron in my life. I had to let Aaron set the pace.

Saturday morning couldn't arrive soon enough. I was really anxious to see him and spend time with him doing something he enjoyed. Running. Who would have thought? I mean, it wouldn't be my personal first choice, but compromise was probably a good step toward building a solid friendship.

Aaron called my cell when he arrived. I made it downstairs in record time to find him out front, stretching. His smile felt like sunshine on this cold, damp morning.

"Hi there. Ready to go? Did you stretch yet? If not, do it now. We'll take it slow at first. Let me know how fast or slow you want to go. Okay?"

"Yes, sir," I teased but began a lunge stretch, mirroring his routine.

"Smartass. I guess I shouldn't be too preachy, but trust me, we won't get far if you cramp up."

"Well, then, I guess we'd have to stop for coffee and breakfast sooner then, right?"

"More like electrolytes and an ice pack. Did you want to grab breakfast after? You didn't say so before."

I looked at him more closely. He'd sounded a little vulnerable somehow when he asked about breakfast. His hair was in his eyes again, though, so I couldn't get a good read on him. I did notice Aaron's attire, though.

It was strange to find myself noticing what he wore and how he carried himself. I'd never paid attention to details like that on other people. Sure, I noticed if someone looked nice, and I would compliment in turn. But Aaron was different. Today he wore those tight black running pants with a bright royal-blue pullover, and again, matching running shoes. The bright blue was a nice contrast to his olive skin and hazel eyes. God, his eyes were beautiful. I noticed his thighs and calves were well-defined. He was muscular but lean. My own running pants felt a little tight suddenly. I had to stop staring at him. What was he talking about? Breakfast? Right.

"Well, sure. You're supposed to treat yourself to a small feast after exercise. Bacon, eggs, pancakes, waffles...."

"Gross! Make it an egg white vegetable omelet or maybe oatmeal and fruit, but never all those bad carbs after a good run! Ugh! My stomach hurts just thinking about it!"

I gave him my best "you've got to be kidding" look.

"So you're saying yes to breakfast, but only if it's oatmeal or egg whites?"

"Sure! Sounds great! Thanks for asking me, Matty. Now let's get a move on."

I was aware this was the first time he'd called me Matty in a long time and that I really liked it. I was also aware that one of us had just played the other. And while I had no idea who came out the winner for breakfast, I felt like it was me simply because he agreed to spend more time with me. I was looking forward to a veggie omelet suddenly.

We ran for about an hour with Aaron chatting the entire way. He was easy to talk to. I asked a question about his workweek and got a colorful, in-depth account of the inner workings of his trade. He had funny stories to tell about power-hungry editors, crazy artistic directors, and poor serfs like himself. The curly-haired girl was a friend of his named Dawn. He told me he thought she had a crush on him, although it was obvious to one and all that he was gay. He talked about other friends at the magazine and then talked about his best friend, Jay, and his partner, Peter. He was entertaining and fun, and I couldn't believe how quickly the hour went by.

I would guess we did about seven miles, and while I was proud I was able to keep up with him, I sensed we were going at a much slower stride than Aaron usually did on his own. Having Aaron doing most of the talking worked in my favor as well. I would have suggested we keep going, but truthfully my legs were feeling a bit rubbery and he had agreed to breakfast, so I didn't have to say good-bye right away.

I directed him toward one of my favorite cafés on M Street and bought us a couple of waters along the way. We sat on a bench outside, drinking greedily while we waited for our table to be called.

"They do serve oatmeal here, don't they, Matty?" Aaron teased. He took a long drink from his water bottle, and hell, that was sexy. My mouth was dry and open. I quickly closed it and took a sip before answering.

"No idea. But I know they have omelets. And bacon, and hash browns, and…."

"Very funny."

"Hey, Matt!" I turned as my name was called to find Jason and Chelsea just exiting the café. I stood up to greet my friends, warning them that I was hot and sweaty and not huggable. Then I turned back to Aaron to introduce him. He quickly stood and shook hands with them.

"We just finished a grueling run," I exaggerated to see what Aaron's response would be.

"Grueling? Boyfriend, if that is your idea of grueling, you need to get out more often. Build up your stamina, ya know?" He winked at me, and I smiled back at him. It didn't escape my notice that he called me "boyfriend," in front of my friends, no less, and I had to wonder what that was about. I was a little slow on the uptake at times, but I was learning that Aaron communicated in a variety of ways. I had a feeling he was testing me somehow.

"So, you guys waiting for a table or something?" Jason asked. "You know...," he suddenly said, turning to Aaron, "you look really familiar. Do I know you? How do you guys know each other?"

"Um, well... we met a few months ago," I started. I hadn't really thought about how I would explain Aaron to my other friends. Not that there was anything to explain. Aaron made it clear we were just friends, but the fact was, Aaron wasn't like any of my other friends. They would be curious.

Aaron wasn't going to help me out here. A glance at him told me it was my story to spin however I wanted. Well, alright then.

"We met at a dance club last year and then I think a bar? But we met up this past week when Aaron was working on a photo shoot for his magazine and—"

"Cool! What magazine do you work for? Are you a journalist? Gosh, I would love to work at a magazine. Is it like *The Devil Wears Prada* or is it a political mag?" Chelsea interrupted, looking genuinely interested.

"Definitely *Prada*, not politics! Although in this town you can't really get away from it altogether."

I watched as Aaron held Chelsea in thrall with a story about the shoot he was working at the other day. His hands moved expressively as he weaved his tale. Chelsea was laughing out loud, looking thoroughly charmed by my companion. I had to smile. I heard a small cough beside me and turned to see Jason giving me a puzzled look. I shrugged in response. I didn't know what else to say. Thankfully our table was called. We'd said our good-byes when Chelsea suddenly turned back.

"Hey, Matt. I forgot. I just ran into Kristin last night. She said to tell you hello. She seems pretty good."

"Great. Tell her hi for me when you see her." I waved a quick good-bye and joined Aaron inside the warm cafe.

We scored a table situated at the enormous bay window overlooking M Street. Perfect for people watching, though I doubted I would notice anyone other than the guy sitting across from me. He was particular about strange things, I was finding. The hostess had set her hand on the chair furthest from the door and indicated Aaron should sit there, probably since he was the first to the table. He obliged, but then sprang out of his seat almost immediately and asked me to switch seats.

"Why?" I was puzzled. We were at the window; both seats were good in my opinion.

"Because I can see the whole café from that seat. You don't care, do you?"

"Uh, no."

"Then switch... please." He batted his eyelashes at me.

I didn't get his logic, but neither was I partial to my view of the café, so I moved for him.

"Thanks, sweetie!" This time I was rewarded with a blinding smile.

"You know, calling me 'sweetie' and fluttering your eyes at me is considered flirting. I'm not sure that's fair of you since we're just here as friends."

"Oh, really? Well, I didn't realize, Mr. Matthew, that you were so in danger of falling under my spell with a simple term of endearment and a facial gesture. I'll try to control myself." He did that thing with his eyes again just as the waitress came to take our drink order.

"So... your friends seem nice." I just nodded in agreement. "I take it Kristin is your girlfriend?"

"Ex-girlfriend," I corrected.

"Right. You mentioned that. When did you break up?"

"Last month."

"Details? Aren't you going to dish? Friends dish! Monosyllabic answers are no fun. Give me the scoop? Was she clingy? Too fussy? Didn't put out? Come on... don't make me guess!"

I laughed because he looked truly irritated with me, and Kristin was the last thing on my mind. I didn't want to talk about her, but I humored him.

"Nothing was wrong with her. It was just me. I wasn't as invested in the relationship as she was." I thought adding that I was interested in someone else, him, namely, might put him off, so I left it at that.

"Cool customer, Matty. I feel for the poor girl."

"I've heard she's been seeing someone new. I'm not worried about her. I think she was looking for a husband, honestly, and I am so not ready for that."

"Ever?"

"No. I definitely want to get married and have kids one day, but I have things to do first. I want to finish my degree and establish myself before I settle down. You know?"

"No. I don't. I've heard that story, but it isn't mine."

"Why not?"

He gave me a "you are so stupid" look. "Really? Well, number one, I'm gay. Number two, I'm gay and not seeing anyone at the moment. And number three, I'm gay and parenting? No, thanks. I have nephews I get to spoil. That's all the kid time I need. I get to be the cool uncle and never have to scold them or clean up after them. That works for me."

"So, what you're really saying is that you would reconsider if you met the right guy?"

Aaron had just taken a sip of the orange juice the waitress had set before him, and he barely managed not to spit it out. He did choke a little, though. I loved that I had gotten to him.

"Very funny. I guess stranger things have happened, and I'm not old. Yet. I may change my mind. Never say never." His tone was upbeat but he was giving me the evil eye, and it was really adorable.

"How old are you again?"

"You are not supposed to ask a girl questions like that!" He scolded in true camp fashion. I caught on that this was an act, so I lifted a brow, encouraging him to answer. "Fine. I'm twenty-eight."

The waitress set our omelets in front of us. Aaron stopped her to ask a medley of questions ranging from a request for hot sauce to what color her lip gloss was. She, too, was thoroughly charmed when she left to do his bidding.

"Why was that so hard? Twenty-eight is young." I looked into his eyes. "Well, young-ish."

"You did not just say that! I am well aware that the big three-oh is looming! No need to add salt to the wound!"

I laughed out loud. He was hamming it up, and yet I could see that a part of him was at least partially serious about the age thing. I couldn't help teasing him a little more.

"You're much older than me, then. Four years."

74

"I know what you're doing, and I won't rise to the bait. Yes, I'm older than you by four measly years, which really just means that I'm wiser."

"No doubt." I smiled at him and he grinned back at me. I held the connection as long as I could.

I was beginning to wonder how long I could remain in the "just friends" mode with Aaron. I wanted him. I was physically attracted to him for sure (the hard-on I had throughout breakfast alone was proof of that), but I also sincerely enjoyed being with him. I had to figure out how to make him want me in return. I thought maybe he was attracted to me. The problem was that he was very wary. I wondered if he'd had a bad breakup or was just not comfortable with the bi thing. This wasn't going to be easy.

As we walked back toward my apartment after breakfast, Aaron chattered about everything from the cupcake store at the corner ("The lines are insane, but the coconut may just be worth the wait.") to a passerby's lack of winter gear (obvious out-of-towner). He was quick-witted and funny. His expressions were hysterical at times, and his hands moved in time with his stories. I had really enjoyed his company, and I was reluctant to say good-bye.

He stopped at a small black BMW parked in front of my place.

"Well, this is me. I need to get home, grab a shower, and...."

"When can I see you again?" Alarm warred with amusement on his expressive face, and I took a second to, again, appreciate how fucking pretty he was. "I mean, as friends." I didn't want to add that last part, but I wanted to make sure he didn't bolt.

"Friends. Well, I don't know, Matt. You know I like to run and go to clubs. I like shopping too, but that look on your face tells me you wouldn't make a fun shopping partner. I know you like sports, but you're out of luck with me there. I know you love music, and you're very good, by the way. You can always invite me to a show. But...."

"Shopping isn't horrible. I could go shopping with you." Yeah, he saw through me right away and held up his hand, laughing.

"Puh-leaze… I can see it now. Ten minutes at Barneys and you'd be crawling out of your skin. But, if you want… well, I mean, if you were interested…."

"What already?"

"There is a photography exhibit at a small gallery off Dupont Circle and…."

"Sure! When?" Desperate much?

Aaron laughed at my exuberance. "It's Thursday night. It's a small exhibit. We wouldn't have to stay for the whole thing, but I said I'd go."

"Cool. I like photography. So, can I pick you up? Do you want to grab dinner after? If you can, I mean."

"Yes. That sounds nice, Matty. Okay, friend, it's a date!"

Affection comes more easily to some than others. I wasn't surprised when Aaron leaned forward to plant a very platonic kiss on my cheek. I was pretty sure I surprised him when I turned quickly to intercept his lips with my own. His eyes remained open, but he didn't pull back right away. His lips were as sweet as I remembered, and I wasn't sorry I'd acted impulsively. It was the first physical contact I'd had with him in two months. My body was crying for more.

Aaron gently pushed me away, his expression telling me he wasn't sorry either. I knew it didn't mean he was ready to move beyond friendship yet, but I made it clear that I was. Time to rein it in, Matt.

"So, I'm sorry. What time did you say?"

Aaron looked at me a little suspiciously but gave me instructions for Thursday, adding that I should dress nicely, but not too nice. I had no idea what that meant, but I would figure it out.

| 5 |

WE TALKED a couple times during the week before our Thursday "date" at the gallery. I took advantage of my wardrobe uncertainty, figuring he'd be the right guy to ask for fashion advice. We were on the phone for a good hour until his battery ran out on his cell and I had to admit to having a paper due the following day.

The next time, it was Aaron calling me. He said he was wondering about a restaurant suggestion for after the show. He warned me they would try to stuff us full of canapés, but we would probably still be hungry. Did I fancy Indian food? I had no idea what a canapé was, and I hadn't had much Indian food but assured him I was game to give it a try. The conversation began while I was making my way home from my internship, through the mass of traffic getting back to Georgetown, and then through a short hike to the market to pick up something quick for dinner. I hung up with him once I was back at my apartment, finishing the conversation as I put away a few groceries. And yeah, I had a big stupid smile on my face.

"Who was that?" Dave had wandered into the small kitchen, chomping on what looked like reheated Chinese.

"Oh, my friend Aaron."

"Aaron. Sweet. When did you meet her?" I gave him a second glance but realized he truly thought I'd met a girl named Erin and wasn't deliberately being a dick. I had no reason to think my friends would know about Aaron, though. I'd kept this, whatever it was, between us quiet. I wasn't sure I was ready to share him, but not because I was ashamed. It had more to do with wanting something real to happen and not wanting to jinx my chances by speaking of it prematurely. Superstitious. Yes, I admit it.

"A while ago, and we're just friends," I explained while I folded my recycle bags.

"Oh. You sounded kinda funny. You know, like you were talking to a hot date, maybe a new chick."

"Mmm. No, not a chick. Who says 'chick' anyway?" Dave just shrugged good-naturedly and plopped down in front of the television.

THURSDAY finally arrived. I whistled my way through two classes and worked three hours at the firm before racing back to my apartment to get ready for my date—correction, my art gallery and dinner outing with my friend, Aaron. He had strongly suggested a nice pair of dark slacks, a sharp oxford shirt ("I know you own one, Matty."), and a dark blazer ("Really optional, but you'd look great in one."). He assured me a tie wasn't necessary. Good. I showered, shaved, and dressed as instructed before swiping my keys off the table on my way back out the door.

Curt and Dave were just coming in as I was about to step out. Dave was carrying a twelve pack of beer, and Curt had what looked like a bag of munchies in his hand.

"Dude! You look nice. Where you going? Hot date?" Dave pushed past me on his way to the kitchen to deposit his goods.

"Um, well actually, I'm going to an art gallery show with a friend of mine." I was tucking my scarf into my nicest coat when I caught the look my buddies gave each other and then me. "What?"

"Who is she, Matt? Come on… you're holding out on us!" Great. Now Curt was curious. That was more worrisome than Dave's questioning. Curt was tenacious. If he wanted answers, he wouldn't stop until he was satisfied. Well, he'd have to wait, I decided. I didn't want to be late picking up Aaron.

"Not she. I'm going with my friend Aaron. See you guys." I escaped immediately, but the look on Curt's face told me he remembered Aaron and that I had some explaining to do. Whatever. I would deal with my friends' curiosity later.

I made it to Aaron's in record time, sending him a text when I was in front of his building. A car was pulling out of a prime spot near his building's main entrance, so I maneuvered my way over to snag it in case Aaron wasn't ready. Aaron called me just as I'd set my car in park.

"Matty, I'm so sorry. I am running so behind. I need another ten minutes. Come on up? I promise I'll hurry. You remember the way?"

"Sure. 5E, right?"

"Impressive. I'm off!"

He sounded winded, like he was indeed in a major rush. I could hear music pumping loudly in the background. Must be his method of unwinding. I smiled to myself, thinking we were similar in that music was definitely how I unwound after a long, stressful day, and yet how different our musical choices were! His dance music made me cringe a little inside, but somehow it made sense to me that it worked for him.

Of course, it came as no surprise as the elevator opened to the fifth floor that the bass boom could be heard down the hall. I shook my head, wondering if he'd hear my knock and how the hell his neighbors put up with him. The door was actually open a bit, possibly in anticipation of my arrival.

"Aaron?" I called over the incessant beat of a Black Eyed Peas song I sort of recognized as I closed the door behind me. I noticed his place was as tidy as I remembered on my first visit; however, a peek into his bedroom just beyond showed a ransacked mess. Wardrobe issue? I couldn't think with the music blaring, and I had yet to see my host. I saw a speaker set up on his kitchen counter and made my way over to put myself, as well as the rest of his building, out of our misery. That caught his attention.

"Oh, hi!" Aaron sashayed into the room wearing very tight black leather pants and a floral-print, blousy-looking button-down shirt. His gorgeous eyes were heavily lined and highlighted with what looked like glitter. His feet were bare, and I think his toes were actually painted to match the black or dark-blue hue on his fingers. He kissed my cheek in greeting and grabbed a small tube of lip gloss, which he used liberally as he took in my appearance.

"You look sexy," he said once his lips were painted to his satisfaction. "I just need to find my boots and I'll be ready to go!"

"Whoa. Wait a sec. I look like I'm attending a conservative gallery opening, and you appear to be going clubbing. I'm a little at a loss here, Aaron." That was an understatement. I had a bad feeling I was being set up again. Aaron, I suspected, had set a scene into play, and I was supposed to figure it out. Fuck it. I didn't mind a little mystery, but he had me unnerved again. Was he attending the gallery show and then ditching me to go clubbing? I didn't think so, because he asked about dinner. I was in over my head, way over my head.

"Don't be silly. You look delicious." I raised my eyebrows at that, and he flashed one of those beautiful smiles at me. I forgot for a second what we were talking about and remembered the last time I'd been here. He must have noticed something akin to desire in my expression, because he looked flustered and quickly busied himself trying to find his boots.

"Are we going to a gallery? I'm confused." My focus returned when he left the room to find socks back in his bedroom.

"Of course. I told Richie I'd go, so I must. What's the matter? Don't you want to?"

"Yes. I'm... I guess I'm a little confused about how differently we're dressed. That's all." It sounded stupid said aloud, but hey, it was true.

"People dress differently all the time, Matt. Self-expression, right? You don't like my outfit?"

He didn't seem overly concerned with my answer, which I guessed was the point. We were different. He made a point of telling me to dress how he assumed I would for an art gallery function (correctly, I admitted to myself) and then dressed as he chose. We were two completely different people, and we looked it. I didn't seem like the kind of guy Aaron would ever look twice at, and he probably assumed he wasn't someone I would be attracted to.

The funny thing was that, in theory, he was correct, but the fact was that I was more intrigued than ever. What else was in store for me tonight? I had a feeling I was going to get a lesson in why we shouldn't try to be more than friends. I smiled at the thought, but felt more determined than ever to change his mind.

Aaron declared himself ready, although when he told me we could walk from his apartment, I did insist he at least put a jacket on. The night was clear and brisk, and the walk was refreshing, if relatively short. Aaron kept me entertained with what I thought were somewhat exaggerated stories of the highs and lows of his day so far. I found myself laughing as he modulated his voice to impersonate a coworker, his hands never still during his tales of life at a midrate magazine, as he so eloquently stated.

We were soon at our destination, a hip gallery near Dupont Circle. We entered what looked like an old brick façade storefront.

The interior, however, was a contemporary surprise. It was completely hollowed out, with exposed air ducts and a super high ceiling. The floors were a highly polished maple, while the walls were bright white and proved a brilliant backdrop to the oversized black-and-white photography gracing them. It was a terrific space. I found myself drawn to the art immediately and interested in the story behind each piece.

Aaron was greeted at the door by a large, redheaded older woman dressed in black and draped in colorful scarves, who literally smothered him into her chest as she kissed his cheek in greeting.

"Darling! You're here! Richie has been asking after you, pumpkin. Go find him and let him know he has friends here. He's so nervous tonight. The usual, I know... and yet, look at this place! Amazing! As usual."

"Oh, I can't wait to see! Gilda, this is my friend, Matt. Matt, Gilda owns the gallery. Richie, I'll introduce you in a sec, is an artist-slash-photographer, and he is always nervous on opening nights! He's very talented. You'll see."

"Pleasure to meet you, Matt. Get that boy a glass of something, Aaron. You're being a terrible friend!" She blew Aaron a kiss and turned to greet guests arriving just behind us.

I followed Aaron into the space and was indeed impressed with his friend's obvious talent. A handsome waiter dressed completely in black came around to offer us a glass of wine. We each took one and turned to gaze together at a large photograph of the New York City skyline. I looked at Aaron, who seemed lost in thought for a moment. I reached over to wipe the smudge of red lipstick from Gilda's enthusiastic greeting off his cheek, and he gave me a weak grin.

"What are you thinking?" I asked him.

"I wish I was there sometimes." He sounded so wistful.

"New York?"

"Yeah. I love it there. Someday, that's where I want to live." He sighed and the longing in his expression said more than his simple words.

"Why? Don't you like DC?"

"Sure. Of course. But, I'm from here practically. I want to see more, do more, you know? I can't see myself on the west coast, but I can definitely see myself in the Big Apple. How about you? If you could live anywhere, where would you live?"

"New York."

He turned to face me, looking like he wanted to give me shit for making fun of him, but he must have seen that I was serious.

"I mean it." I shrugged in response. "I'm from a small town outside of Pittsburgh. I love this city. Don't get me wrong. But once I have my law degree, pass the bar here, and have a couple of years of experience with a reputable firm, I want to move on and see if I can make it there. The ultimate challenge, so they say, is New York City. 'New York, New York.... If you can make it there, you can make it anywhere'," I quoted.

Aaron mustn't have expected such an impassioned speech about NYC from me. His mouth was literally open in astonishment. I went on complete impulse, figuring I'd apologize if I had to, and leaned forward, placing a chaste kiss on his mouth. He closed his eyes when our lips met, and I took the invitation, deepening the kiss and closing my own eyes, momentarily lost in Aaron. Until someone came up behind us and coughed loudly. Aaron started and jumped away from me in surprise.

"Richie!"

"Hi, baby! So happy to see you! Who did you bring us?"

I couldn't help but be a little irritated at Richie's interruption, but I could tell upon meeting him that he wasn't the type you could stay angry with for long. He was smiling at Aaron in obvious adoration, but he was so much older that I took it to be a fatherly sort of look and not pervy. He was a few inches shorter than Aaron, and if I had seen Richie's application of makeup before I'd seen Aaron's eyeliner and gloss, I wouldn't have even noticed Aaron was wearing any. Richie was decked in colored eye shadow, blush, and lipstick. He was dressed more like Aaron, in tighter-fitting black jeans and a black velvet jacket with a hint of a fuchsia-pink T-shirt underneath. He looked genuinely happy to see Aaron and equally happy to meet me. I smiled in return and offered him my hand in greeting.

"Hi, I'm Matt. Aaron's friend. Your photography is absolutely incredible. I'm so glad Aaron invited me tonight." I knew I was probably laying it on a little thick, but he appeared to appreciate it and Aaron was giving me the sweetest shy smile, so I figured I was doing the right thing after all.

"Thank you. So very nice to meet you, Matt." Richie shook my hand enthusiastically, smiling all the while. He winked at Aaron and then turned to kiss his cheek. I thought I heard him say something like, "Don't let this one get away, honey," before he turned to greet other patrons in the now-crowded gallery.

We made our way through the exhibit, sipping wine and commenting here and there on Richie's artistic vision. I learned that Aaron had met Richie when he taught a class on photography at the university Aaron attended. They'd been friends for a few years now. I was introduced to his partner, Dean, as well, who was Richie's polar opposite. Tall and robust, he looked a bit like a gangster from an old Humphrey Bogart movie. In fact, I thought maybe he meant business partner until I caught Dean's arm move protectively around Richie's shoulder in a lover's embrace at one point. It made me smile. Things aren't as you assume.

I couldn't help but notice the exhibit's attendees were almost all gay or lesbian. I had never been introduced to so many partners outside of a law firm. The patronage ranged from very effeminate to very masculine for both male and female. Aaron kept an eye on me,

I'm sure, gauging my reaction. I wondered if he thought I'd be scared away by the rampant homosexuality in the room. Honestly, I found it liberating in a way I couldn't quite explain.

"Are you hungry, or did you have one too many canapés?" Aaron asked as we left the gallery.

"Canapés are hors d'oeuvres, right? I ate a couple, but I'm starving. Do you still want Indian?"

Aaron laughed. "Yeah, Indian sounds great. Curry chicken would be divine right about now. What did you think of the exhibit?"

I had enjoyed the gallery much more than I imagined I would have, and I told him so. Aaron grinned up at me happily. He began weaving another story as we walked, complete, of course, with hand gestures. This time it was about Richie and what his photography class had been like when he taught Aaron at university. I was ultra-aware of Aaron's arm brushing against my own. The streets were busy, and we were jostled together more often than not. I was actually grateful to have the excuse to touch him. He'd have been surprised to know I loved being in the gay-friendly part of town, where touching another man in public wasn't anything out of the ordinary. If anything, I wished he'd let me hold his hand. I decided, "What the hell?" and grasped hold of his fingers when his arm swung down again. He smiled at me in surprise, but he didn't pull away.

The restaurant was small, and if I hadn't been with Aaron, I would have passed right by the entrance. He let go of my hand, pointing to the door.

"This is it. It doesn't look like much on the outside, but don't judge yet." And with his customary flourish, Aaron held the door open for me.

The restaurant's interior was dark, but there were brightly colored lanterns hung throughout the space and beautiful printed pillows at each booth. The table we were shown to had a single lantern and a red rose on it, giving it a cozy, romantic vibe. I wondered how this all fit with our "friend" status, but wasn't stupid enough to ask.

"This is nice," I commented after we'd placed our drink order.

"I know. I love this place. Can't eat Indian all the time, but this is absolutely my fave. You want to share some curry chicken, or do you not do sharesies?"

I laughed out loud. "Sharesies? You are funny. Yeah, I'll sharesies with you, but order a lot of whatever. I am starving. Those canapés weren't much."

"Ha-ha... very funny. Make sport, if you wish. I'll do the ordering Paul Bunyan style for my manly friend here. I just can't...." Aaron stopped midsentence as someone vaguely familiar approached our table.

"Aaron! Hey, honey, how are you?"

No way. It was the bald guy I'd seen him running with last month. The one who kissed him on the street. I could feel my blood begin a slow boil. Who was this guy, anyway? I knew I was giving our unexpected visitor a less-than-welcoming stare and was surprised by the depth of my jealousy. I could feel it like a physical thing. Aaron seemed to take it all in stride. I noticed he seemed a little cool to our unwanted guest but then again, maybe it was wishful thinking on my part.

"Hi, Chris. I'm good. You?" Yes, definitely cool. I was hoping to get the full story as soon as Mr. Clean left. Geez, man, take the hint. Go!

"Good, good. Um, hey... I don't want to interrupt. Enjoy your dinner. I'll call you?" His expression was a little hangdog and pathetic, but I didn't feel the least bit sorry for the guy. Now I was just curious. How did they go from the sexy smooch on the street to Aaron basically giving him the "I'd rather never see you ever again" brush-off?

Chris gave Aaron one last supposedly meaningful look and finally turned to leave. I couldn't see who was with him, but it didn't seem the kind of restaurant you came to alone. Curiosity was eating me, warring with the haze of jealousy the unwanted visitor had inspired. I was sincerely hoping my chatty companion wouldn't disappoint.

Silence. Total silence.

Oh fuck. That meant he meant something to Aaron, right? Maybe he was nursing a broken heart and messing around as "friends" with me was supposed to help cure it? This could be a nightmare.

I was startled from my reverie by Aaron's giggle.

"You should see your face!" More giggling. What the hell?

"What exactly is so funny? And who was that?"

"Lower your voice, Tarzan." His eyes were still sparkling in amusement, but I was still in the dark. Plus I'd seen them together... I knew there was a story here!

"Well...," I prompted.

"Chris is just someone I used to know. That's it."

You've got to be kidding me. That fiery feeling was taking over again. *He cannot seriously leave it at that.*

Aaron laughed out loud this time. "What is with you? Oh... I think someone wants to dish. Am I correct?"

"If you mean I want you to tell me who the hell he is and why he was looking at you like that, then yes... please, dish."

"Oh my, you're jealous! Wow." He held up his hand as I sputtered and tried to deny it. "That's very, very flattering. Fine. I'll tell you as one friend to another. Okay?"

In other words, he didn't owe me an explanation but was choosing to give me one. Fine by me. For now.

"Chris is a nice guy I used to see once in a while. I broke it off with him at the beginning of the year. Remember me telling you that

I made a New Year's resolution or two? One of them was to stop getting involved with men who are bad for me. Like Chris."

"Did he do something to you? Did he hurt you?" I sounded like a thug. Like I was going to go after him and kick the guy's ass if Aaron confirmed anything abusive had gone down. But I couldn't help myself. I couldn't control my reactions to Aaron. I felt insanely protective toward him.

He smiled warmly at me, telling me with that one sweet gesture he appreciated my overreaction. Then he continued dishing.

"Not physically, silly. Chris is like many men in this good old capital of ours. He's a married-with-kids closet homosexual who likes to play when he goes away to work in the big bad city. My resolution to myself was that I won't be the asshole he's screwing around with, yes, bad pun intended, while his wife is changing diapers back home in Nebraska. I'm not going to get involved with anyone ever again who isn't 100 percent out and gay and proud to be with me."

I was reeling from the first part of his speech, and when I tuned back into the second part, I got the full picture of who he thought I was.

The worst thing was he wasn't—or hadn't been—half-wrong to assume I wasn't an out-and-proud gay man. But what he didn't realize, or maybe what I still needed to show him, was that I wanted to be out for him. I wanted a chance, and I was pissed now, knowing that jerk had set me back just by being the asshole he was. No wonder Aaron insisted on us just being friends. He was probably sure I was looking to get my bi-curious experience on with him and dive back into the hetero side of the pool. I didn't know how to prove myself, but I was determined to do so.

"Whoa. Okay. I won't ask any questions, but can I please ask that you don't ever, ever—" I paused, trying to gather my whirlwind thoughts. "—don't think I'm like him. I'm not, Aaron. I... look, this may be a crappy time, but...."

"Don't. Please. You'll ruin my curry chicken. I don't want to think about Chris. I'm sorry we ran into him. But let's leave the rest alone for now. Please?"

What could I say? I agreed. Dinner was a bit more subdued than I thought it would have been if we hadn't run into Chris, but by the time the check came around, Aaron seemed like himself again. We argued over the bill and I won. I was rewarded with a huge smile and a kiss on the cheek as we headed back by foot to his place.

I was hoping he'd invite me upstairs, but I didn't know how he was really feeling about running into his old "whatever he was." Truthfully, I wanted more information. How did Aaron get involved with a married man, anyway? I tried not to dwell and instead focus on Aaron's new round of chatter, which was all about food. Did I cook? No. Was my mom a good cook? I thought so. What was my favorite home-cooked meal? My mom's lasagna. And on it went.

I learned that Aaron professed to be a rather good cook, if he did say so himself. Nowhere near as accomplished as his mother or his sister, Maria, but better than his sister Tess. And don't make him laugh, but his father and brother couldn't figure out how to boil water together. I was a little like his dad and brother, so I didn't comment there. I loved how he talked and shared little pieces of himself. I was sure he didn't think he was doing anything but filling the silence; however, he was actually telling me about himself and the things and people he cared about, like his family. He obviously adored them all, but seemed to be a little distant with his dad. Probably not totally surprising, since it sounded like his family was a traditional Latino one. Catholic and all, he told me.

By the time we were back in front of his building, we were both laughing over one of my failed cooking exploits dating back to grade school, when I had attempted to make my mom breakfast in bed for Mother's Day. Runny eggs crunchy with shells and burnt toast. Yum. The condition of the kitchen probably would have earned me a sore bottom if my heart hadn't been in the right place. Aaron was wiping tears away as he laughed at my poor younger self.

It made me smile. I could not figure out, for the life of me, why this eyeliner-and-lip-gloss-wearing raven-haired male beauty was turning me inside out, but I was smitten. Truly, utterly smitten. If I had to regale him with embarrassing stories of my youth to stay with him a few minutes longer, I would gladly do so. Lord knows there was no shortage of embarrassing moments to draw from.

Aaron regained his composure, and a comfortable quiet fell over us as we stood next to my car. I gave into temptation and reached out to run my fingers through his hair. He took another step toward me as our mouths met in the middle, fusing and twisting in a passionate kiss. He licked my lips, inviting me to taste him. I thrust my tongue in his mouth, tasting the curry mingled with a sweetness that was Aaron's alone.

"Upstairs?"

I nodded in agreement, almost positive I couldn't speak. He took my hand and led me up to the main door, then unlocked it with a steady hand before capturing my hand again and drawing me toward the elevator. We kissed gently while we waited for the elevator, and then inside the car to the fifth floor. Once we were outside his door, he fumbled with his keys, trying to work the lock. I nibbled at his neck and licked his ear while I waited.

"Want me to do that?"

"Mmm. Got it." He unlocked the door and closed it quickly as we fell inside, tangled up in arms, tongues, and fingers.

I wanted to feel him, touch him. I'd never done more than kiss him, really. He'd sucked my dick, and I'd yet to feel him naked against me. The hunger to do so was overwhelming. I wanted him with a fervor I'd never felt for anyone before. Our lips pressed together as we worked off our jackets. I felt his fingers fumble with the buttons on my shirt, and I reached for him, struggling to do the same for him with trembling hands. I was nervous but sure. I got the first few undone and felt him smile against my mouth as he took over for me and undid the rest of his own buttons. I moaned as I finally felt his bare chest with a shaky hand. He worked on my buttons next, and we both groaned in pleasure as our naked chests met. He moved his hands over my back, caressing and then scratching as he fought to get closer to me. I felt them dip to my belt buckle, and I reached down to redirect him toward his own. I had to see him and touch him, and whatever else he would let me do tonight. He complied, gesturing for me to do the same.

"Wait. Bedroom," he instructed. "Oh… shit, it's a mess. Hang on."

Aaron broke free of me and hopped toward the bedroom. I groaned at the loss of his touch but was equally happy to get horizontal with him. I certainly didn't care if the room was a mess.

And it was. There were clothes everywhere. He'd obviously had a hard time deciding what to wear tonight. I laughed when I saw him swipe carelessly at whatever was on top of the bed to create a place for us to lie down. He scowled at me but went back to the task. I lay down on his dark-gray sheets when there was a space for me. Aaron moaned in appreciation.

"Get naked."

"Not until you do. I need to see you."

I know I made one of those gulp noises when he began his striptease. It was the sexiest thing ever. His shirt was long gone, probably back in the living room, but I watched in awe as he slowly unbuckled his belt and went straight for his zipper. His abs were beautifully toned, and he was slender without being too skinny. He swayed his hips and then turned away from me. I made a noise of protest until I saw the globe of one of his bare ass cheeks. He'd gone commando. Fuck. I had to get my jeans off while I still could. I was so hard, and precum was dripping from my cock at an alarming rate. I did not want to embarrass myself by coming just from watching him undress. I worked myself free of my jeans, but he stopped me with a noise and a shake of his head, telling me not to lose the briefs yet. I gulped again but did as instructed, folding my arms behind my head to watch him.

He shook his ass as he shimmied the leather over his beautiful bubble butt. He bent over from the waist down, giving me a full view of everything I hoped he was offering. I was probably panting by now and my heart was beating halfway out of my chest.

Aaron smiled seductively at me as he turned to face me, showing himself to me for the first time.

"Fuck. You are beautiful." I didn't realize I'd said that out loud until he responded.

"So are you. So are you," he purred, and then came toward the bed and straddled my legs.

He was gorgeous. There was no other word. His skin was the most beautiful shade of olive everywhere. No tan lines visible. His cock was rock hard like my own. It looked a little smaller in size and girth, but it was perfect on him. I ached to feel him in my hands. I reached for him, but he pushed my hands up above my head and held them there.

"Please. I have to touch you." I was begging.

"You will. Just let me get these off you."

He let go of my hands and hooked his fingers under the waistband of my briefs. I shifted my ass off the bed so he could remove them. He pulled them down my legs and bent his head to lick the head of my cock at the same time. I pushed my hips up toward his mouth instinctively. Fuck. I would not last at this rate.

"Aaron... please."

"What is it? What do you want?" He was hovering over my cock with his tongue, making catlike licks on the head. Then he swallowed me whole. My hips shot forward and a cry sounded in the room. I pushed him off me.

"Aaron. Fuck, baby. Please. Stop."

He leaned away from my dick, back on his knees, and I rose up quickly to meet him and kiss him breathless. I rolled him sideways, pushing him on his back before lunging on top of him. I was trying not to overwhelm him with my desire, but my control was worn thin. I leaned back, supporting myself on one arm as I looked at the beautiful naked body beneath me. I ran my hand over his abs and pinched his nipples. He whimpered and arched into my touch. I explored lower still, running fingers along his hip and cupping underneath his ass. I purposefully ignored his cock, though I knew he had to be aching the same way I was. Leaning back, I took my right hand and licked a swath of spit across it before finally wrapping my hand around his pulsing, swollen member. He gasped and writhed in pleasure when I moved over him, bracing myself on my left arm while I grabbed my own cock, then rubbed them together and created a mind-blowing, blissful friction. I was trying my hardest not to be the first to come.

"Open your eyes." I did as he asked and felt my balls tighten and rise. I couldn't wait any longer. I came so hard and so long, my body shook with the effort to stay upright and ride out the aftershocks.

"Baby, come for me." I felt him fall apart under me, his cum coating my fingers as he moaned through his release.

"Fuck."

I fell over to his side, struggling to catch my breath. That had been earth-shattering and we hadn't even fucked. God only knew if I'd survive it.

I looked over at Aaron, noticing he'd gone quiet, and wondered if that was cause for alarm. He had a peaceful look on his face, but it gave way to a Cheshire-cat grin when he felt my gaze on him.

"You look awfully pleased with yourself," I commented.

"Hmm. Yeah, maybe so."

We turned toward one another, lying on our sides. No words were said. I didn't want to break the spell. I didn't want the night to end. I had no idea what the rules were from here on out. Of course, I couldn't leave well enough alone.

"I want more than friends, Aaron." *Shit. Why did I say that? He'll freak.*

Aaron turned onto his back and stared at the ceiling. He didn't answer for long minutes, and I was just starting to think maybe that was my answer.

"I guess it's stupid to pretend I'm not interested, Matty. The problem is that you may not be that guy that I swore I was done with at New Year's, but you really fit the mold on paper, and I just don't know if I can deal with it." He turned to look at me, and although I wanted to plead my case, I kept quiet while he finished his thoughts. "Can we go slow? Just… I don't know, just slow?"

"Yeah. Slow is good." I knew all the joy I was feeling at that moment was written all over my face. I wanted more, and I wanted it fast, but I would go slow for Aaron.

We held each other and explored one another through another round of orgasms, but this time the pace was slow. In deference to our new agreement, I thought. Whatever it was, I knew I would be waking up with a smile on my face. Reluctantly, I crawled out of his bed, kissing him before I headed out.

| 6 |

I MADE it through the next day on a caffeine high. I had one class at nine and a three-hour stint at the law firm before I was free for the weekend. Scratch that. Before I was free to study and catch up on my assignments. I had four months of law school left. I couldn't afford to fuck it up. There wasn't anything pressing going on other than an almost physical urge to spend time with Aaron. But I promised myself I would give him space and time.

I called him on my way home from the city. I couldn't take it. I needed to hear his voice.

"Hey there." He sounded happy to hear from me. Good sign, right?

"Hi. I just wanted to hear your voice." *Fuck, I shouldn't tell him the truth.*

"Oh... Matty, you are sweet. I like hearing your voice too. We never got around to talking about it, but what are you doing this weekend?"

"Honestly, I have a ton of school work to get through. I'm devoting my weekend to it. I can't afford to get any more behind than I am."

"That would be bad. Well, if you can get away from your books for a teensy while... would you like to join me and a couple of friends for brunch on Sunday?"

"Sure!" was my immediate response.

Aaron laughed at my timing and then explained that he tried to get together with Jay and Peter at least a couple of Sundays a month for a mimosa-infused brunch. He claimed not to be a fan of a threesome with a naughty chuckle, and was hoping I'd join them this weekend. I agreed to be their fourth.

"Cool. Plus, I want you to meet them. I have to run. I'm still at work, and I have a feeling I'll be here another few hours."

I had just stepped up to my front door and was loath to end the connection without at least acknowledging the night before.

"Okay, I'll let you go, but I just... I wanted to tell you...."

"Yeah, me too."

"It was amazing, Aaron. That's all I'll say... promise. See you Sunday, okay?"

We hung up, and I fumbled to get my key out of my pocket just as another hand reached out to unlock the door. Curt. Shit. He gave me the look. The one that let me know it was time to start explaining. I knew I didn't owe anyone an explanation, but somehow I realized this could be a good way to start the coming-out process. "Coming out" sounded ominous, but if anyone could give advice I might be willing to listen to, it would be Curt.

"So... how much did you hear?"

"Enough. Are you with him, like *with* him? It is Aaron, right? What's going on with you, Matt?" Curt was flustered, and I have to admit his concern made me feel guilty, like I'd kept something from him that was vital. I didn't want to ruin my high with guilt, but I decided I would answer what I could.

"I like him, Curt. Like him a lot... like him." I was smiling, so I was sure he could read between the lines of my junior high-school explanation.

"But what's the deal? Are you gay? Bi? Gay for him? I don't understand. I mean, in my world, gay is gay, and you, my friend, have never exhibited any signs of being remotely interested in dick."

I busied myself looking at a stack of mail piled on our entry table, keeping my eyes averted while I spoke.

"Look, I'm bi. I guess. If we have to label it, that's what it is, I suppose. I was with a guy once before, a long time ago, but he wasn't important to me and I chalked it down to an experience. This is different, Curt."

I turned to face him. I wanted him to know I was being sincere.

"How? Maybe it's an every-five-year thing? No offense, dude, but there is nothing worse than a straight guy who likes dick once in a while in secret, of course, and then pretends he wouldn't stick his pole anywhere near another dude if they were the last two horny, able-bodied people left on the planet."

"Fuck you, Curt. I am not like that. You know me."

"I do. I think I do. I know you're a good guy and you're my friend. I'm just trying to understand."

"I can't explain. I met him at that dance club last year. Remember? Dave and Jase and I went with you."

"Yeah, I remember. And I remember meeting him again at that bar a couple weeks later. I know who he is."

"What the fuck does that mean? What do you mean you know who he is?"

"Down, boy. I'm just saying this is a small gay community, relatively speaking, and Aaron isn't exactly a wallflower. I'm not suggesting he's not a great guy, but I do wonder what the fuck you expect from him. Ideas? Do you want a boyfriend?"

"A boyfriend? Geez, man. I don't know. I don't know how to categorize or say what I want, because honestly, I don't know." There went the last of my high. Crash, burn, bam. Damn Curt. It was a good question. Aaron asked the same thing in his own way. He didn't say it in so many words, but I understood that he questioned my motivation. What about me? I knew I wanted Aaron. I wanted to talk to him, be with him, listen to his stories, kiss him, touch him, and yeah, I really wanted to fuck him. What then? Did I want a boyfriend? I'd never considered it before now.

"Never mind. I do know. Yes. I want him. I want everything with him. No hesitation. Right now I'll take what I can get. He wants to go slow, so I'll go slow, but the truth.... The real truth, Curt, is that I want whatever label makes it so that I get to be the guy he calls first for any and every thing. I want to be someone to him. Does that make any sense at all?"

"You're serious? Are you in love with him or something?"

"Why do you go straight to the L-word? It's too soon to say shit like that. And I sure as fuck don't want to scare him away. But man, Curt. I can't breathe around him sometimes. I just want to stare at him. He's so fucking beautiful. And he's funny and sweet. I love his laugh and yeah, I love being with him. That's all I got right now."

"That's a lot, man. More than most."

Curt looked a little shaken by my speech. I noticed neither of us had taken our jackets off since we'd entered the apartment. I slid mine off my shoulder, hung it up, and went to the kitchen to grab a couple beers.

"It's all the crap that comes along with this that freaks me out, but I'm going to try not to overthink. I feel like I've been going through the motions for way too long and I finally *feel*, you know? I'm not giving this up."

"I wish you the best. You know that, right?" I nodded and thanked him. "Does this mean you're 'coming out'?" Yes, he did air quotes.

"I guess. Aaron is out, and I don't think he ever knew what a closet was, other than a place to store clothes, so yeah, if I want him, I have to be honest and open about it. I'm not going to lie and tell you that doesn't terrify me a little, actually a lot, but... I think he's worth it. I just need to go slow too."

"I'm not suggesting he isn't worth it, but let me ask the question you don't want to... what if it doesn't work out? Still worth it?"

"I think if I just make it about being honest, with myself and the people who care about me, then the answer is yes. If it doesn't work out, I still need to be able to say I was honest and I went for it. All I can do is try."

"Well, cool. So, do we get to meet him officially sometime, then?"

"Absolutely. Just let me work on convincing him I'm what he wants before you scare him away." Curt flipped me off, took a swig of the beer I'd brought him, and finally took his jacket off.

I HAD arranged to meet Aaron and his friends on Sunday, at what Aaron claimed to be the very best of the best french toasteries in all of DC. Plus he claimed the mimosas were to die for. I was pretty sure there was no such thing as a french toastery, but I took the hint that it was what he would be ordering and if I had a brain, I would do the same. I'd have to ask him about the exception he was making regarding his carb intake. I remember him insisting on a vegetable-laden egg white omelet last time we ate breakfast together.

Sunday turned out to be a true winter day. The sky was gray when I left Georgetown and seemed to get darker the closer I got to the bistro where I was meeting Aaron. The weatherman called for snow by early afternoon. It seemed like a safe prediction to me. I was dressed in full winter gear, complete with a beanie cap, in preparation for the elements. I was born and raised in a state where a winter storm is something to be taken seriously. DC is technically the South (which I believe every humid summer without fail), and the winters have proven mild while I'd lived here. Somehow I couldn't shake the habit of preparing for wicked weather, even when I was sure we'd get a couple flurries and that would be that.

I unraveled my thick wool knit scarf, searching the small French-modern interior of the restaurant for Aaron and his friends as I made my way toward the hostess desk. I was chilled and more than a little grateful the bistro was warm. Aaron spotted me and waved me over to a table situated near a corner window. There were two extraordinarily good-looking men sitting with him. Jay and Peter. Geez, he hadn't mentioned they were hot.

I admit to being a little nervous about meeting these particular friends of Aaron's. I knew these were people who mattered to him. I couldn't help feeling self-conscious as I approached the table.

All three stood at once. Aaron gave me one of his glorious smiles in greeting. I felt myself begin to relax when he grabbed my hand and leaned forward to kiss me softly on the lips. God, he tasted sweet. I could taste the champagne on his lips. I smiled down at him and then turned as he began a flurry of introductions, his hands flying in time with his words.

"Matty, this is Jay, my best of all best friends. And Peter, Jay's partner, lover, boyfriend, whatever you want to call it... also my friend, probably because he's stuck with me. And guys, this is Matt."

Funnily enough, it sounded to me as though I wasn't the only one nervous here. Aaron's intro was certainly his style, but a little more manic than normal, which made me think he wanted them to like me too. The thought made me smile. He did care. Cool.

I shook hands with both men before taking my seat next to Aaron, who was busily calling the waiter over to order another round of mimosas. Another round? Peter groaned and reminded Aaron he was working that afternoon. He called the waiter back to cancel his second mimosa, ordering coffee instead. I took advantage of the diversion to study him and Jay.

Peter was tall, dark, and classically handsome. I would guess one of his parents was Italian. His cheekbones were high on his chiseled face, his skin a light shade of olive, and his stubbled chin had the slightest of dimples. Not overwhelming or cartoonish, just sexy as hell. The guy could have stepped straight out of a GQ fashion spread. And Jay would absolutely be the model standing next to him. He was equally hot in a completely different way. Where Peter was classically handsome, Jay was East-Coast-prep-school-boy sexy with dark-blond hair and golden skin. I noticed when they stood to greet me that both men were tall, easily matching my own height, if not a little taller.

Aaron had talked about them, certainly, but I don't think he mentioned looks. I felt intimidated by their beauty, which was a strange thing to even admit to myself. I knew I was generally considered a good-looking guy, probably along the lines of a basic all-American jock, but these guys were special. However, if Aaron considered them special, it was obviously for more than their appearance. Aaron liked pretty things, sure, but I knew he wasn't the type to hang around pretty guys with no substance. His love of his friends, particularly Jay, was evident in how he spoke of them.

"So, Matt, Aaron's told us just a little about you. You're a law student?" Jay's question snapped me to attention.

"Yes. I'm graduating this year, taking the bar, and hopefully will be hired on at the law firm where I've been interning for the past year."

Peter asked about my internship. He explained that he dealt with some of the partners at my firm through his work as a lobbyist.

Jay volunteered that he and Peter had met at work. Peter, Jay gushed, was a genius at his profession, while he himself had never really enjoyed working for a large company. Jay was in the process of establishing in own business as a consultant.

Conversation revolved for a while around work-related topics. I found Peter to be a cool customer. He was friendly but appraising, as though he was withholding judgment. Jay, on the other hand, was effusive and affectionate. His gracious, amiable manner was much like Aaron's. It was easy to see how the two were best friends.

Jay eventually asked about how Aaron and I met. I was pretty confident Aaron had already told him the story, but I figured he was curious to hear my version.

"We met at Club Indigo back in October." I was blushing and feeling unsure about how to continue. Jay must have sensed my discomfort. He smiled gently and began to tell the story of how he and Aaron met at a dance club years ago. BP. Before Peter. Peter rolled his eyes, but gamely sat back and listened to a story he obviously knew well. He looked on at his partner with exasperated adoration. I was charmed, and I hadn't even heard the story yet.

"Aaron is a seriously amazing dancer, am I right? The thing is, he knows it. What was the name of that club, A? Do you remember?" Aaron supplied the name, and Jay was off again. I heard a soft Southern lilt in his voice as he warmed to his tale. I wondered where he was from originally.

"Anyway, there's this hot Puerto Rican boy out on the dance floor of a club, mind you, that I've been to a million times and have never once seen. He is dancing sooo sexy. This guy...."

"Eric," Aaron helped, his eyes twinkling with mirth as he sipped his mimosa.

"Yeah, Eric the asshole. I remember. He tells me to check out my competition. There's a new boy in town, he just turned twenty-one, and all the men are drooling. So of course, I'm curious. I turn my head in time to see Aaron, shaking his thing and dazzlin' the crowd. I went straight for him, thinking this cute sweet thing probably would love to meet a slightly older man who can shake his own thing."

"Ha! Yes, you see, Jay knows how to move too, and he is not shy. I remember you practically rushing me and bumping me out of the spotlight so you could take your rightful place as god of the boogie."

"Well, whether it started out as competition on my part, I don't recall, but we danced literally until they kicked us out. And we kept it super sexy, remember, honey?" Jay drawled.

"Did you guys go out? I mean...." I was sure Aaron would have mentioned that Jay was a former lover. I got that queasy jealous feeling at the thought.

"*No*, silly! My Jay is a beautiful boy, but we realized right from the start that we are friend material only, not boyfriend material. We had so much fun that night, and I guess the rest is history."

"These two prima donnas would certainly make an interesting couple." Peter laughed as he massaged the back of Jay's neck.

"Oh, screw you. We are not prima donnas. We just have more discerning tastes than some. Isn't that right, Jaybird?"

Jay leaned over and planted a kiss on Peter's cheek. They were a cool couple. They seemed to complement one another well. Peter, with his laid-back, appraising manner, and Jay, with his charming, sweet nature. I liked Aaron's friends. It was great to meet people who knew him and cared about him too.

The gray skies from earlier were delivering something more than a few flurries by the time we left the bistro. I slipped into my jacket, wound my scarf around my neck, put my beanie on my head, and looked over at Aaron to find him woefully underdressed in a long cashmere coat without a hat or scarf.

"You can't be serious? You are going to freeze," I protested.

"What do you mean? This is cashmere."

"Yeah, so now your cashmere coat is going to get wet in the snow. And where is your hat? Your scarf?"

Aaron tilted his head to one side, giving me a puzzled look.

"I'm fine. We're just going to the car anyway."

I fished my hands into the inside pockets lining my jacket and found an extra beanie. It was black-and-yellow striped with a Pittsburgh Steelers logo. A Christmas stocking stuffer from my folks, probably.

"Here. Put this on." I reached out to Aaron, who gave me a quick sidestep.

"You must be joking. That is hideous. It's a teensy bit of snow, Matty. I'll be fine."

"Put it on."

I wasn't budging. He either sensed my resolve or was conscious of his friends watching our exchange. He stepped toward me, giving me and my beanie cap a dirty look. I ignored him as I placed the cap on his head, tucking stray strands of his hair underneath. He kept his eyes on me while I fussed over him, making a show of pulling the hat well over his ears. He looked part sexy sophisticate in his beautifully tailored coat and part feisty little boy with the football-emblazoned cap and pouty look on his face. I couldn't resist giving him a light peck on his lips. He looked surprised at the public display, but didn't say a word.

"Matt, are you dropping Aaron off for us? Peter has to go into his office for a bit." Jay and Peter were barely stifling their laughter at Aaron's put-upon expression.

"Of course." We exchanged brief good-byes with Peter and Jay outside. The wind made it difficult to linger, and it was clear Aaron was indeed chilled. His teeth were fully chattering by the time we reached the relative warmth of my car. I drove cautiously back to his place, which was thankfully nearby.

"You're coming up, yes? I have to give you this horrible hat back, and although I hate to admit it, I want to keep it on my head for as long as possible. I'm fucking freezing."

I laughed and assured him I was happy to walk him in and take the offensive garment with me when I left.

"Good. As a reward, I'll make you a cup of tea."

We hurried inside. I took over opening his apartment door when his hands shook from cold and he couldn't get them still enough quickly enough for either of our comfort.

"Geez, Aaron! It's cold in here too." I walked in after him, unraveling my scarf, but had second thoughts about removing much more. His place was barely warmer than outside.

"I know. I try not to heat it at night and when I'm not home. These old places are expensive to heat. If I knew it was going to be this cold, I wouldn't have bothered saving a couple of bucks."

He removed his coat, but not the cap, on his way into the kitchen. I could smell his cologne when he brushed past me, something spicy but subtle. I followed him into the small space, and moving behind him, gently laid my hands on his hips. I pulled back the cap over his left ear with my teeth and kissed his earlobe, breathing in his scent. I was acting on impulse. I wanted him, not the tea.

"Me? No tea?" Aaron turned to face me, looping his arms over my shoulders.

I grabbed the cap from his head and buried my nose in his hair, his ear, his neck. Anywhere I could get close quickly. I was ravenous for him. I heard him moan my name as our lips finally met. The pull of desire was strong. A wave of longing washed over me, urging me to take more. My hands were moving of their own volition. I needed to feel his skin against my own. Our tongues twisted and danced in a building frenzy. Aaron broke for air first.

"Bed." He took me by the hand and pulled me out of the kitchen. I paused for a second to shrug off my jacket and hat. Aaron moved ahead of me, removing clothing and seductively dropping each piece in his wake. I was literally salivating at the first peek of his skin. I caught him around the waist, licking and kissing the back of his neck as we stumbled into his room.

The bedroom was equally chilly, but I noticed the bed had been made and everything was clean and tidy. No scattered clothing lying about this time. The queen-size bed with a dark, modern wood frame dominated the room. There was an end table on one side of the bed and a dresser, all of the same dark wood, that doubled as the second end table on the opposite side closest to the window. The walls were painted a light shade of gray, but the comforter on his bed and the pillows were a bright, cheery red with bright-colored striped accents. It was a tasteful space. Masculine but colorful. Like Aaron.

He pushed me backward onto the red comforter and climbed over me, showering my jaw and neck with kisses and bites. I let my arms fall back over my head and gave him control. He gave me a mischievous smile as he clasped my hands in his and rolled his groin over mine. The feel of his hard-on through our clothes left me breathless with need. I flipped him over, delighting in his gasp of surprise. I ground my jean-clad dick into his. We both moaned at the pressure and pleasure. It was almost painful.

"Off... take these off. I want you naked." I could barely get the words out. Thankfully he was feeling the same sense of urgency. I backed off of him to allow us both to remove belts, jeans, shirts, boxers. Clothes went flying as we hurried to press our naked bodies together. It was bliss. I knew if I wasn't careful, I could come just rubbing against his beautiful body.

Our tongues met again as our hands roamed freely over one another. I ran mine down his back, over his hip, and cupped his gorgeous bare ass. He arched into my touch and bit my shoulder lightly before licking me over my collarbone, up my neck. His hands were in my hair before he took a detour down my back. His touch was potent. I was breathless and aware of my own need to slow things down a notch. I rested my forehead against his, trying to calm myself before my cock exploded prematurely.

"Slow down, okay? I want you so bad, Aar. I'm about to lose it. Show me what you want me to do." I placed a soft kiss on his swollen lower lip.

"I want you too. You can do anything you want." He writhed underneath me and forced his hands between us to grasp both of our cocks together. Precum was dripping between us.

"Fuck! I'll come if you don't stop. Please. Can I…? I mean, do you want to…?"

"Fuck? Is that what you're asking me? Yeah, Matty. I want you. I want to feel you inside me. Fuck me."

I audibly gulped and closed my eyes. I couldn't remember ever feeling so turned-on and yet so in over my head. I was in new territory here. It had been so many years since my last sexual encounter with another guy, and that was a drunken one. This was real. I wanted this with every fiber of my being, but I didn't know where to start. I wanted to make him feel good.

Aaron's eyes were ablaze with the same desire I felt, but he must have noticed my uncertainty.

"We don't have to do anything you aren't comfortable with, Matty," he said earnestly.

"No, that's not it." I groaned in frustration. I wasn't good at the talking about feelings anyway, but I couldn't let him think I didn't want this. "I want you so bad, but I… fuck, Aaron. I don't know what to do. Show me how to make you feel good."

Whatever I said was obviously the right thing to say. Aaron beamed at me as he ran his fingers through my hair.

"I can do that," he whispered sweetly as he gave me a gentle shove. He leaned over the bed, fumbled in his nightstand, and came back with a condom and lube. My heart sped up again. I could feel it trying to beat its way out of my chest.

Aaron opened the lube and poured a generous amount in his hand as he lay back against his pillow. He positioned his right hand under his ass cheek. I watched, mesmerized, as he lifted his right leg and exposed his hole, his finger breaching his opening.

"Can I?" I whispered. I wasn't sure he heard me, but he handed me the lube and nodded.

I put some on the fingers of my right hand and then gently rubbed them over his hole. His finger was inside but he moved it, allowing me to take over. I let my middle finger slip inside, feeling the warmth within. I glanced up at him to make sure he was okay before I slid a second finger in beside the first.

"Move them, Matty. That feels nice." I did as he asked. Aaron's eyes were half-closed. He shifted his hips to ride my fingers. It was so wanton and sexy. I placed my other hand on his cock and stroked it as I fingered him. He closed his eyes, moaning my name.

"Stop." I reluctantly obeyed, stilling my hands. "Your turn, Matty. Lie down."

Once I was on my back, he knelt between my legs and cupped my balls with one hand. He slid his other hand up and down my cock slowly. It was a teasing touch I was sure was meant to torment me. I looked down at him just in time to see him lick the length of my erection before taking it whole into his mouth. My hips jolted off the bed.

"Fuck, Aaron!"

He sucked me harder, moving his right hand in time with his tongue and hollowing out his cheeks. He made a mumbling noise that reverberated along my dick, sending shivers up my spine. I rolled my head from side to side. The pleasure was intense. He kept a firm hold of me as he reached for the condom and used his teeth to unwrap it before sliding it down my turgid cock. I felt the cool lube through the condom as he coated it once more before moving up my body and straddling my torso.

"We'll go slow. At least at first, okay?"

I could only nod in agreement. Speech was beyond my capabilities at that point. I felt Aaron place my cock at his entrance. My breathing was erratic and a sheen of sweat broke out all over my body as he slowly lowered himself onto me. The look on his face was pure rapture. I placed my hands on his hips but let him control the pace. He watched me closely as he shifted his weight forward, creating friction for his cock trapped between us. I was deep inside him now. It was pure ecstasy. Aaron licked my mouth, requesting entrance. We kissed and he quickened his pace.

"Can I touch you?" I could feel his hard cock leaking on my belly.

"No. I want to come when you do. Get on top of me." I groaned as he slid off of me, missing his weight.

Aaron lay flat on his back with his legs spread wide. Fuck, he was beautiful.

"Matty, please. Fuck me."

I positioned myself between his thighs and pushed inside him. I heard myself whimper at the feel of his heat wrapping around my cock.

"You feel amazing. So good, baby."

"Do it, Matty. Fuck me hard."

I needed no other encouragement. My hips rocked into him repeatedly. His legs were wrapped around my hips, his arms around my neck, and our mouths were at each other's necks. He smelled so potently male. It was intoxicating. I felt my balls begin to draw up and knew I was close.

"Baby, I'm gonna come." I held myself up on one arm and looked into his stunning hazel eyes before I came apart. Wave after wave crashed over me. I heard a shout but wasn't sure whose it was. I felt Aaron's body shudder beneath me as his orgasm overtook him as well.

I couldn't move for the life of me, but I was probably crushing my partner. I braced myself on my forearms and took a long look at our bodies fused together with sweat and semen. Aaron was watching me through hooded eyes, probably trying to gauge my reaction.

"You okay?" I asked.

"Hmm. Yes. Better than okay," Aaron purred, running his tongue over his bottom lip. I traced the same path with my own tongue before I gently pulled out of him. I made my way to the bathroom, flushed the condom, and grabbed a washcloth. I ran warm water over it before returning to my lover's side. I carefully wiped the come off his chest and the lube from his hole.

"Thank you. Lie here with me, Matty. Are you okay?" Aaron's voice was soft in the aftermath of our love. I caught a glimpse of snow lightly falling outside his window as I joined him under the covers. He rested his head on my shoulder and closed his eyes.

"Better than okay."

And I was.

We spent the remainder of that Sunday in his bed, alternately talking and fooling around, just naked kissing and touching. We were warm and snug wrapped in the big red comforter and in each other. A perfect way to spend a cold winter afternoon. When one of our stomachs protested that there had been too much activity without sustenance, we reluctantly gathered up our discarded clothing and made our way out into the now-dark living area.

"How about a sandwich or, let's see… I could make a veggie omelet?" Aaron stood barefoot, staring at the contents of his refrigerator. He had opted for comfort, changing into a pair of sweats and a tight-fitted T-shirt. I fought the urge to tell him he should put some socks on. His apartment was still a bit cold even with the heater turned on.

"Whatever you feel like making is good for me. Want any help?"

"Well, if you'd like a glass of wine, you could pour one for both of us."

He showed me where to find glasses and a wine opener while he presented a bottle of pinot noir.

"Everything goes with a pinot, I always say." He turned his attention back to gathering ingredients for an omelet while I poured the wine.

"I say that about beer, but this is good too." I winked at him and offered a toast.

"I'm not a beer drinker. Too many calories for something I just never really got a taste for. I tried to like it in college, but I couldn't get there. Ended up drinking shots of tequila before I realized it was out 'to kill ya'," he quipped, making a silly face.

I almost spit the pinot out. I was sure his wine appreciation didn't extend to showering the veggie omelet. His joke wasn't particularly funny, but his timing and the expression on his face was unexpected and endearing.

"That was bad. Warn a guy, would ya?"

"Impossible! I'm unpredictable, Matty. Who knows what I'll say next?"

We both chuckled softly. Aaron suggested I turn on some tunes. I knew we didn't have the same tastes in that realm, so I asked what the chef requested. With the faint sounds of music in the background, I studied my companion busily sautéing veggies and cracking eggs. It was a homey, comforting atmosphere with easy company.

Aaron brushed his hair from his eyes, using the back of his hand to do so. His sweats hung low on his hips, accentuating the curve of his delectable ass. I'd never been the type to stare at a lover before, to just take in their beauty. But I found myself admiring his small, fit form, beautiful eyes and skin. I watched his graceful movements and felt a rush akin to gratitude that we had physically connected. It seemed like an over-the-top sentiment, but a true one nonetheless.

"Are you sore?"

Aaron looked over at me in surprise as he folded a huge omelet onto a plate. He turned to grab utensils and napkins before waving me toward a seat at his small kitchen table. I took my seat and another sip of wine while I waited for my host to join me. The omelet looked fantastic. I was famished.

"Cheers!" Aaron toasted as he finally found his chair. "And the answer is yes, I am a little bit, but don't freak out. It's normal. Anyway, I'm one of those weird guys who likes it." He winked at me before turning his attention to divvying up our dinner.

I was glad I hadn't taken another sip of pinot.

"Huh? What do you mean? I hurt you, didn't I?"

"No, idiot. I'm trying to tell you, it was fabulous. But it's natural to feel a little sore afterwards… for the bottom, at least. And feeling it is a total turn-on to me. No more questions. Eat. No, wait…."

I waited for him to continue for a few quiet seconds. He looked agitated and I was beginning to worry.

"Look, Matt. I need to know something."

"What?"

"Are you okay? I just need to know if you're going to freak out."

I wanted to pretend I didn't know what he was talking about, but he deserved honesty.

"I'm... I don't know how to describe what I am, other than... definitely not freaked out. Aaron...." I hesitated. Words failed me, yet I knew I had to try to communicate. "I feel alive for the first time. I know that sounds ridiculous. Maybe it's the result of post-orgasm euphoria, who knows? I just feel great. I can't promise that this whole—" I waved my hands between us when again I lost the words. "—us... doesn't freak me out a little. I'm being honest. I just know that it feels right. You feel right."

"You too, Matty."

We ate in silence, staring at one another over the rims of our wine glasses with Adele serenading us softly. I gave into impulse, leaning over to place a chaste kiss on his sexy mouth.

"Thank you. This has been a really amazing day."

Aaron rewarded me with one of his glorious smiles. Yeah, it was a great day.

| 7 |

WINTER passed a bit more mildly, with cool days and chilly nights. But other than a flurry of snow to complement the occasional rain, it looked like a safe bet that spring would be timely. I saw Aaron as much as possible. We were both swamped with work, and I still had school and a bar exam to prepare for. If we didn't see one another, we talked on the phone or sent texts daily. He sent me silly messages that left me with a goofy smile on my face a few times a day. Curt caught my shit-eating grin a couple times and gave me an inquisitive look, but I didn't share. I wasn't embarrassed or ashamed of my new relationship or whatever it was Aaron and I had. I was protective of it. I didn't want to share him with anyone else. The time we had together was special. We still saw our own friends, but more and more often, I spent at least one night of the weekend at his place. He lived alone, so there were no explanations required. Plus we could be as loud as we wanted.

My roommates, of course, noticed I wasn't sleeping in my own bed on weekends. I decided to just answer with the truth. Or at least a half-truth.

"I met someone."

"Yeah, Einstein. We figured that out. Who is she?" Dave asked one late Friday afternoon in March. I had stopped by my place to shower and change before going over to Aaron's. He was having a few of his friends over. He claimed it would be very low-key, but I was feeling a little nervous nonetheless. I hoped Peter and Jay would be there.

"Aaron."

"Erin…." Dave drew the name out like he was talking about a porn star. "When do we get to meet her?"

I raised my eyebrows, grabbed my bag, and made a speedy exit. Half-truth. I got angry with myself for not telling Dave and Jason about Aaron, but the whole situation was new to me on so many levels. Aaron was so full of life, easily excitable, and charming. I wasn't sure what he saw in me. We didn't have much in common on paper. Our tastes in music, movies (he loved romantic comedies, of course), and hobbies were polar opposite. However, we never ran out of things to talk about. He loved to debate the merit of what made something or someone interesting, be it a musician/pop star or a politician. He was well-informed and well-read. I suppose I was attracted to his intelligence and the fact that he was an avid learner. If he didn't know or understand something, he researched it so that the next opportunity he had to debate, he was better informed. He asked me questions about cases I read about or that I might be involved in someday. It was intoxicating to be with someone who always seemed interested in you. Aaron was intoxicating. And fucking beautiful.

He opened the door for me, wearing the tightest leather pants I think I'd ever seen on him, with a designer-label blousy white shirt with only a couple buttons fastened. His hair was disheveled, like he'd just blown it dry but hadn't bothered with product, his feet were bare, and yeah, he looked sexy as hell. I swallowed loudly, making him laugh with pleasure as he took the wine bottle I'd brought from my hand and danced away, leaving me staring after him in the doorway.

The music was blaring. Some techno-pop mix that set my teeth on edge. I needed a drink and to get to the volume control without him noticing. I did both while he finished primping in the bathroom.

"Bad boy! I can't hear a thing!" Aaron reemerged looking even more gorgeous. His eyes were sparkling with amusement. Thankfully, he didn't readjust the sound. I had poured him a drink, which I handed over quickly to keep him distracted.

"Thank you. What? No hello kiss?"

He leaned toward me, offering me an exaggerated kissy mouth. I laughed. When our lips met, though, he licked a seductive trail along my lower lip before opening his mouth to mine. We moaned in unison, our drinks forgotten. We were interrupted by his cell phone playing a Lady Gaga tune. He laughed and skipped away to answer it while I adjusted myself and picked up my cocktail.

As he answered the phone, I watched his expression go from pleased to exasperated and maybe a little hurt within a few minutes. He had switched from English to Spanish. Maybe family? The conversation wasn't long, but it had left him deflated. I moved toward him, wanting to offer comfort or an ear if he wanted to talk. However, the doorbell buzzed before I had a chance. In an instant, I watched Aaron transform his features from angry and hurt to gracious and welcoming host. All traces of his earlier distress were gone as he opened the door for the first of his guests.

Aaron had invited six people for a small dinner party. I'd already met Peter and Jay, so that meant four other of his close friends would be joining us. He'd left work early that day to prepare the food himself. His theme was Puerto Rico. Every party needed a theme, according to him, and he'd been completely mortified to hear I didn't know if I'd ever eaten Puerto Rican food. I figured it was probably like Cuban or Mexican, right? Wrong. And after Aaron got over being insulted by my ignorance, he decided to cook a traditional Puerto Rican feast to enlighten me. He claimed he was scaling it back a bit, but from what I could tell, there was a ton of food prepared and ready for eight of us to enjoy.

The first guests to arrive were a young man named Ben and his older boyfriend, Mark. There had to be easily ten years difference between them. Ben looked to be younger than me. He was stylishly dressed in tight black jeans and a slim-fitted black V-neck sweater. Aaron commented on his Goth look, which earned him a halfhearted slap on the arm and a grin from Mark. Mark was nice looking in a professorial, unassuming way. I later learned he was a professor at American University, which is where the two met. Aaron had told me they'd been together forever. I wondered what their story was. Ben worked at the magazine with Aaron, and they'd known one another through work for a few years.

Katie, Jay and Aaron's best "girl" friend, was next to arrive, with a guy named Glen. Aaron obviously adored Katie. He fawned over her choice of outfit and gushed over her handbag. She was pixie small, with long auburn hair and a fair complexion. Her features were sharp, a pointed chin and heart-shaped face with high cheekbones, but they suited her. Poor Glen barely got the time of day. Apparently Aaron and Jay didn't bother getting to know her boyfriends because they didn't stick around for long. Katie was fun and boisterous. She seemed a little wary of me, but since I was new I took it as a normal reaction of a protective friend.

Jay and Peter rounded out the party. They were the last to arrive. Aaron didn't seem surprised. Peter made a comment about them being on "Jay time," so I assumed late was his norm.

Aaron outdid himself in the kitchen. He accepted help only from Jay and Katie when he was ready to present his masterpiece Puerto Rican fare. He'd made a few dishes using plantains and a rice and chicken dish called *arroz con gandules* with a secret sauce called *sofrito*. Everything tasted amazing, and I admitted I was more than a little impressed with his culinary expertise. Jay made a batch of sangria to complement dinner, and before long everyone was relaxed and enjoying themselves, perched around the living room coffee table. It was homey and comfortable. I tried to help clear away plates but was ushered out of the kitchen with a kiss from the chef.

It was a nice evening. I liked Aaron's friends. Conversation was easy at dinner and everyone was friendly and outgoing. I had been talking friendly politics with Mark in the living room when it occurred to me I hadn't seen our host in a while. I excused myself and made my way to the kitchen, stopping to pick up a depleted pitcher of sangria. I rounded the corner and found Jay with his arm around a visibly upset Aaron. Aaron had tears in his eyes and it looked like Jay was comforting him. The rest of the party was chatting in the living room, oblivious to any upset. I was a little confused by the turn in his mood. He'd seemed fine all evening.

"Hey there. You okay?"

He wiped his cheek and gave me a reassuring smile.

"Yes. I'm fine. Jay was telling me a sad tale."

Jay looked at Aaron for a long minute before excusing himself to check on the masses for the host. The look was one of silent communication. My immediate reaction was irritation, but obviously something had bothered Aaron earlier and he'd confided in Jay. That was probably natural, but I couldn't help wanting it to be me comforting him.

"Tell me, babe. What is it?"

"I will. Later, okay? I promise it's nothing big. Just the frustrating norm."

"Promise?"

"Yeah. Come on. Let's make sure they aren't reorganizing my DVDs."

I watched Aaron closely after that exchange in the kitchen. The only thing I noticed, though, was how much he was drinking.

The guy was downing sangria like he might never get another glass. I knew there was a potential for real danger, however, when Ben brought out a bottle of Patrón. I'm not a big drinker, really. I tend to stick with beer or the occasional glass of wine or a vodka tonic. Tequila just makes people do stupid things. I wasn't going to partake. Besides, I wanted to keep a watchful eye out for Aaron. He had brushed off his party hat and was definitely ready to wear a lampshade. One of us should be halfway sober.

An hour later, with the lights either dim or off, the small apartment resembled a small dance club. Someone had a Rihanna song playing so loudly the speakers were vibrating. Shot glasses littered the coffee table, and Katie was dancing up a storm with Jay, Ben, and Aaron. I stood next to Peter, wondering where this night was going. Suddenly, Aaron stopped dancing and ran over to turn the music down so he could be heard.

"Okay, friends! Shot time! And then clear them away! It's time to dance on the tables!"

Aaron got busy serving up another round of tequila while I looked on helplessly. I turned to Peter to get his reaction to the drunk-fest.

"Matt, my friend. Sometimes, you just got to go with it. They are way too hard to handle when they get like this. Trust me, Aaron and Jay are bad enough together. With Katie in the mix, it's a done deal. A hurricane. Just wait for it to run its course."

Katie's date was trying to hang with the four dancers, but Mark, Peter, and I retired to the kitchen area, taking turns trying to keep the music at a reasonable volume. One of his neighbors had already knocked on the door. When the same neighbor came by, Peter and I assured him there was no need to call the police. Peter took over, turning on the lights and suggesting they maybe unwind with something less noisy. I had to admire how he handled them, making it sound like it was part of their itinerary. Aaron squealed in delight.

"Great idea! Wii!" Katie, Jay, and Ben were in, except there were only two controllers.

"Rock, paper, scissors to see who plays first." Jay was practically swaying on his feet, but Aaron, Katie, and Ben were game to keep going.

I found myself back in the kitchen with Peter and Mark, sipping from a bottle of water while we listened to the rowdy group egging one another on playing video games.

"Are they always like this?" I nodded toward the other room.

"Not always, no. I suspect someone needed some cheering up and the other two came to the rescue. It's how they work. Ben is just being a good sport." Peter craned his head around to check on his partner. "We'll let them run out of steam and get out of your hair."

"Not my place. I'm cool."

"Maybe not, but if you aren't staying with Aaron, then Jay and I should probably stay the night. Aaron is going to be sick, judging by the amount of alcohol that kid consumed tonight."

"No, I'm planning on staying. I just meant you didn't have to run. If you want to stay, that's cool too."

"No, I'd rather sleep in my own bed. Just checking to see how the wind blows here. You like him, don't you?" Peter didn't necessarily look surprised that I really liked Aaron, but maybe he wasn't expecting me to take on the mess that was surely coming when Aaron sobered up.

"Yes. I like him. A lot," I confirmed, taking another long swig from my water bottle.

Mark sighed heavily, as if bracing himself.

"Well, we are getting out of your hair, so to speak. I'm tired. I'll get Ben and see if we can give Katie and her guy a ride home too."

I straightened away from the counter and offered Mark a hand.

"Great to meet you, Matt. Aaron is a great guy. A handful, maybe, but a great guy." He shook my hand, said good-bye to Peter, and left to round up some drunks.

I hoped he was successful. Truthfully, it had been a long day and I was tired. Plus there is something about returning to a sober state when everyone around you has moved on to inebriated. It was exhausting.

Mark had Ben by the arm and was directing him toward the door. He somehow talked Katie and Glen into joining them. He must have convinced them they were off to another party because they certainly didn't look ready to stop. Jay and Aaron had their arms around one another and were laughing hysterically as they waved to their buddies. Fuck only knew what the joke was. I caught Peter's attention and rolled my eyes at our dates.

Peter and I made small talk and cleaned up a little bit while Jay and Aaron sat on the sofa doing a rendition of "man, you're so my best friend." They seemed to alternate between manic mirth to heartbreaking melancholy and back again.

I was stacking some glasses into the sink when Jay came into the kitchen, looking for Peter.

"Where's Aaron?"

"Passed out on the sofa. Keep your eye on that one, though," Jay warned me with a hiccup. "He is foxed!"

"And you aren't?" Peter brushed his fingers through Jay's thick dark-golden hair, making Jay purr like a kitten.

"Take me home, lover. I am 'xhausted!"

"Yeah, I bet. Let's go. Good luck, Matt."

FINALLY, they were all gone. The only sounds in the apartment now were Aaron's soft snoring with Pink singing about being sober in the background. I tried to nudge Aaron awake, but he was having none of it. He twisted away from my voice, curled into a fetal ball, and put a pillow over his head. Okay... this was going to be difficult.

I went back into Aaron's bedroom, turned down the sheets, and then went back to scoop him into my arms. I gently laid him in bed, taking off shoes, socks, and belt and undoing his leather pants. He rolled away from me, impeding further progress. I gave up for a minute, deciding to lock the place up and grab him some water and aspirin. I thought about getting a wastebasket to put next to him just in case he didn't make it to the toilet, but I knew Aaron was particular enough to not dare get sick on his own high thread count sheets and comforter. I finished undressing him and took care of myself before joining him in bed. I kissed his sweaty forehead before tucking him in.

At 4:00 a.m., I heard retching noises from the bathroom. I was going to let him be because, come on, who wants to be around a puker? But the soft sobbing wasn't something I could ignore. I bounded out of bed to find Aaron on his knees, huddled over the porcelain bowl. I grabbed a washcloth, and after wetting it with cool water, I knelt beside him, dabbing his forehead. He flinched and began crying in earnest.

"Hey there. It's okay. You're alright," I soothed. He looked fucking miserable, which I suppose he deserved. I couldn't help feeling sorry for him though.

"I'm sick. Don't look at me. Go away, Matty." He was sobbing, leaning over the bowl and waving his arms behind him. Pathetic. Obviously he needed me, though. I wasn't going anywhere.

"Hey, it happens to us all. Take a sip of water. Come on. Now let's get you back to bed."

He insisted on brushing his teeth, so I stood silently beside him, ready to give a hand in case he slipped or stumbled. He was definitely unsteady on his feet. I had to physically take the toothbrush from him, tip his head back to take a small drink of water, and then lead him by his waist back into bed. He was asleep before his head hit the pillow. Me? Not so much. I spent the next hour at least watching over him. Making sure he wasn't going to vomit in his sleep and choke to death. Fuck! What a night.

The funny thing was that, in spite of Aaron's late drunken spiral, it had been a very entertaining evening. Something had definitely gotten to him before the party, and of course I knew it was the phone call. It was cool he had friends like Jay and Katie he could confide in, but I found myself once again wishing it were me.

The next morning, I woke up to the sun casting a bright streak across the bed. I was alone in Aaron's bed. Ugh! I checked my watch to see it was nine o'clock. I called out to Aaron, wondering if he had made any coffee. He certainly needed it, and I could use a caffeine infusion myself. I stretched out and was about to hop out of bed when Aaron came shuffling slowly into the room. He had put on a pair of boxers and a T-shirt. His hair was mussed up from sleep, and the dark circles under his eyes were definitely not all the result of leftover eyeliner.

"I'm... I don't have... can't find coffee, Matty."

I laughed, although truthfully, I wanted to cry. He just looked so damn cute. Pathetic but cute.

"So we'll go get some."

His stare was desolate. Alright, time to be a real hero. Attending to your puking date was all well and good, but saving us both from a morning without coffee after the night we'd had? Priceless.

"Okay, okay. I'll get some coffee. Be right back."

I got dressed quickly before I could change my own mind. I was back within half an hour, after stopping for some croissants to go with the coffee. The look of complete and utter joy when I handed him his extra-large coffee was all the thanks I needed. We sat at his kitchen table, drinking our coffee and eating the pastries. Well, I ate mine. Aaron just picked. He was in for a rough day.

"You going to tell me what's bugging you?"

"Please tell me it wasn't obvious. I know Jay knows me well enough to know when I'm uptight, and Katie too, but I was hoping no one else caught on."

"It was the phone call, right?" He nodded sleepily. "You're tired, babe. Want to talk now or go back to bed and try to get some more sleep?"

"I want you. I am tired, but I still want you. You're a good man, Matt. Thanks for taking care of me last night."

"Come on. Let's go back to bed and just lie there for a while. You look like you're still in recovery mode."

"Bed, yes. It's going to be a recovery day, I know. But I still want you."

I remember thinking my passion for him should have been at least a little tempered by recent events. I mean, for fuck's sake, the guy was worshipping the porcelain god a few measly hours ago, and then was literally in tears about the coffee situation, which I had had to rectify. But no, I wasn't bothered by any of it. If anything, I was happy to take care of him. He brought out a strange new protective side of me. And when he told me he wanted me? Well, my dick didn't require any more encouragement.

We stripped our clothes off as we made our way to the bedroom. Of course Aaron insisted on brushing his teeth again. My mouth watered at the sight of his sexy ass as I watched him from the bed. He asked how I managed to get his tight leather pants off him the night before. I assured him it was not easy. We both were laughing pretty hard at the picture of me struggling to unpeel him from his sexy pants. They had been really tight.

"I shouldn't have had seconds." He snorted while trying to stick out his small belly.

When we were both naked under the covers with laughter still lingering, we stared into each other's eyes. All amusement was abandoned as we came together, skin to skin, savoring one another's touch. I entered him slowly, making love to him gently. I could have wept with the sweetness of it. I had never felt so connected and one with a partner. A wave of feeling, so strong I was weak with it, made me wonder why everything was so much better with Aaron.

I WOKE up with his head on my chest. He was softly snoring, his hair in his eyes. I stared at him, taking in his long eyelashes and his sleep-mussed hair. The eyeliner from the night before was still streaked across his lower lids. His smudged eyes reminded me of a cute little raccoon.

"What are you looking at?" he mumbled as he stretched in my arms.

"You. You look like a little kid with that makeup all over your eyes. An adorable little raccoon." I kissed the end of his nose.

"You're mean." He wiggled away from me and made his way to the bathroom to clean up before making a dive back into my arms as I lay waiting for him.

"No fair. I need to at least brush my teeth," I grumbled as he pressed kisses over my chest, stopping to play with my nipples.

"Alright, but be quick. You look mighty tasty this morning, Mr. Sullivan."

I laughed as I left his side to take my turn in the bathroom. I took a moment to study myself in the mirror before heading back to bed. Did I look different? I'd never felt better. I wondered if it was obvious to anyone else.

Aaron was checking messages on his phone in bed. He didn't look up when I got in beside him. I noticed his brow was furrowed and wondered if whatever had bothered him yesterday had resurfaced.

"Somebody buggin' you? You don't look as relaxed as you were a few minutes ago." I snuggled into his side, attempting to divert his attention.

"Yeah, you gonna beat him up?"

I propped myself on my elbow, lying on my side to get a good look at his expression. What was going on? Did that guy Chris come back in the picture? He hadn't said a word about any other guys while we'd been seeing each other. I never pictured having this conversation with a guy, but the idea of anyone else touching Aaron set my blood to an immediate boil. I didn't want to share him. I was going to have to broach the subject no matter how uncomfortable it made me.

"Who?"

He must have heard the hum of temper in that one word, if the raised eyebrow and questioning look he tossed at me were any indication.

"Down, boy. Just family stuff. My dad. Same old story. I wish it didn't bug me. Sometimes I'm sure it doesn't at all anymore. But then something stupid just gets me. Fuck! I'm just an idiot."

"Hey. What happened?" I calmed down instantly when I realized I couldn't actually kick his dad's ass. It was time to put my jealousy aside and listen.

"It's just family shit, Matty. I should be used to it, and for the most part I am, but he still gets to me."

I waited for him to continue. He lay flat on his back, staring at the ceiling for a minute or two before speaking.

"In my family, my culture, being gay is difficult. My mom, my sisters, and even my brother are fine with it. But my dad is very old-fashioned. He tries, but he doesn't always succeed, if that makes any sense." He turned on his side to face me. "If I had to be gay, I think he wishes I could be more like you. You know? You're masculine, like sports, and generally don't appear to like other men in a physical sense. I'm not that way."

"I'm glad. I like you just the way you are." I ran my hand over his side and the curve of his hip.

"Hmm. Well, that's good, because I don't know how to be anything else. I mean, Matty, I've been me, this me, since birth. My dad used to blame my older sisters, saying they treated me like their little living doll. They'd dress me up in their clothes, our mom's high heels and makeup. I loved it! They weren't doing anything I didn't absolutely adore. Trust me, my brother is two years younger than me and he was always all boy. He would have thrown a fit if they tried playing dress up with him. Not me, though. They would tell me how pretty I was, and I loved it. My mom thought it was funny, but my dad... not so much. Anyway, fast-forward twenty-odd years and he still struggles. Sometimes I sense that he really tries, but it doesn't change the fact that I'm a disappointment to him."

"Don't say that."

"Matt, you don't know. Like I said, it's partly a cultural thing and partly a total machismo thing. My dad is a macho Puerto Rican man with very old-fashioned ideas about the place of a man and a woman in a household. A gay son? Embarrassing."

"Did he hurt you? I mean...."

"No. He's not like that. He's fair. I mean, I got in trouble the same as any kid. It's just that the relationship we have isn't anything like the one he and my brother share. My dad coached his soccer teams growing up. They both love sports. Especially baseball. Me? I have nothing to add there. I never liked sports. I did track and field in high school and college, but team sports were not my thing."

"So, what happened last night? Did he call you?"

"No. I'd called my mom earlier to check on a recipe I tried last night. When she called me back she asked me who was coming over and I heard him make some comment in the background about it being a fag party. I doubt he thought I could hear him, but his hearing is getting bad as he's getting older and he doesn't realize how his voice carries. It's no big deal. Nothing I haven't heard many a time before, but fuck... every once in a while it gets under my skin. And that is the worst part. Knowing I'm letting stupid ignorant words hurt me. I'm better than that. I just hate that my dad still says them. He'll never change. In his own way, I know he loves me, but it just hurts."

I pulled him close to me and held him tightly in my arms, as though my hold would keep his hurt at bay. He melted into me. I felt the warmth of his tears on my chest and held him closer still.

Aaron was right. I had never had to deal with any name-calling, or worse, because of my sexuality. Hell, no one knew I was bi or gay. I didn't dress, act, or speak in a manner suggesting I liked men. I knew, of course, that was stereotyping, but that stereotype had enabled me to keep my own secret for a long time. I had been comfortable in my relationships with women, but I had never felt fulfilled. Sexually, being with Aaron was like discovering the real me. I was still me, though. I still loved playing and watching sports, loved hanging out with my buddies. I didn't think that would change when they found out about Aaron, but I couldn't deny that I would be hurt if it did. I hadn't even thought about my family. They were good people, and I knew they loved me, but I wasn't ready to think about the repercussions of coming out to them.

Aaron wiped at his face and cuddled into me. I kissed his tears away and made him laugh when I jokingly told him I was going to kick his dad's ass. I tickled him until he was hysterical and finally let up when he wiggled out from under me, straddling my thighs. We were gasping for breath as we stilled our playing. Then Aaron swooped down to lay flat over me, wrapping his arms around my neck in a sweet embrace.

"Thank you, Matty. You're my knight in no clothes." He sighed and laughed softly in my ear.

I smiled into his hair. Knight. Yeah, that sounded fine by me.

| 8 |

SPRING in DC was truly beautiful. The cherry blossoms came into full bloom, creating a picturesque landscape in the capital. Aaron sent me a text one Saturday morning in early April, giving me his "photoshoot" location. I had no idea what that meant. With Aaron, one could never be sure. It could mean anything from he sent me a text meant for a coworker and they were to meet for a work-related shoot or he had some adventure or another up his sleeve. The heart-shaped emoticon, I decided, was meant for me. So I sent him a return text asking if I needed running shoes. The swift reply was "not unless you plan on running away from me!" He added that he would explain when I got there, and to hurry.

I met him at the Tidal Basin near the Jefferson Monument, as instructed. The West Potomac Park was covered in cherry blossom trees in bloom. It was stunning. I took a moment to enjoy the scenery while I waited for Aaron to arrive. There were tons of people out and about. The day was overcast, but the sun was making a valiant effort to break free of the clouds. I spotted Aaron near the monument, with a tripod and a large camera draped over his neck. He was wearing a pair of aviator sunglasses and a leather jacket. He looked like a sexy pilot. I laughed at the image I'd conjured and made my way over to my handsome companion.

"Hi, Matty! You're here! Isn't it unbearably gorgeous?" He gave a flourishing wave at the trees and pond.

"Yes, you are."

"Oh, stop. No, go on." We stared at each other, letting a silly silence pass between us. Aaron broke my stare first with one of his beautiful smiles. "I have decided a day like today is the perfect day to brush the dust off this old, well, not too old, Nikon and take some scenic photos. Please say you'll let me take your picture!"

"What? No. I mean, it's cloudy, right? Not a good day to take photos."

"*Au contraire*. The cloud cover makes it *perfecto* for my purposes, as I won't have to worry about glare. You look handsome as ever, but I'm actually not planning on doing any close-ups. More silhouette. Okay?"

I begrudgingly agreed. I moaned and tried to suggest other, sexier things we could be doing with our morning, but Aaron would not be dissuaded. He meandered to a quieter part of the park and set up his tripod. I felt a little unsure about what he had in mind here. I stuffed my hands in my pockets, my shoulders nearing my ears as I waited for instruction.

It came by way of "move to the left," "turn sideways," "perfect, Matty." In other words, I just stood around and he took a steady stream of photos. How anyone could be a model was beyond me. I was restless, and the only thing that kept me from running away was the look of utter excitement on Aaron's face. I hadn't seen any of his work, but if he simply took joy from taking photos, maybe that was all he needed.

"Okay. Now, let's maybe find another angle," the artist mused, looking seriously about.

"No offense, babe, but let's do something else for a while. How about I take a picture of you?" I whipped out my cell phone and started shooting pictures of him with the built-in camera feature.

"No! I'm a mess! Matt! Oh, whatever, at least I have sunglasses on."

He hammed it up for me, making me laugh at his silly faces. I kept right on taking pictures until he'd had enough and made a run for me. I'm a pretty fast runner, although I admit Aaron is faster when not burdened with a heavy-duty Nikon around his neck. He dashed after me, but kept missing. When he'd had enough, he literally sat down cross-legged on the grass and pouted until I stopped. He looked like a child not getting his way. It was hysterical. I held up a hand in truce, but the second I got close to him, he pulled me down beside him and jumped on top of me. I halfheartedly wrestled him off me. We were both laughing and breathless when Aaron called uncle.

"Geez, Matty. Pick on someone your own size!"

"Okay. So now, what do you want to do?" I stood up, dusting off my grass-stained jeans. I offered Aaron a hand up. He looked around thoughtfully and a manic light came to his eyes. Uh-oh... another idea.

"No more photos, please?"

"Better than that! Let's go on the paddleboats!"

I'm sure my blank look said it all. That was for tourists, not residents. I really didn't want to go on a paddleboat. I looked toward the great pond that President Jefferson's statue presided over, framed by glorious cherry blossom trees. Oh yeah, and a ton of out-of-towners intent on taking in all of DC's treasures in a weekend. I turned back to Aaron to tell him exactly what I thought of that idea, but I couldn't do it. The look in his eyes was all excitement. Once again, he reminded me of an over-eager little kid.

"What about your equipment?" It was my final attempt at avoidance.

"My car isn't far. I'll go put it in the trunk and voilà... we're good to go! What do you say, Matty?" He fluttered his eyelashes at me. Seriously.

"Cut it out. Alright! But you owe me for this one."

"I'll pay, don't worry!"

"I don't mean money, honey." I tried to give him a stern look, but his smile was too big for me to hold on to my mock anger.

"I don't either! Come on, honey. You carry the tripod. I'm this way."

I found myself following after him, wondering how I got here. He had me doing stuff I wouldn't usually agree to in a million years. Paddleboats? I was still trying to think of an out when I looked ahead to see Aaron practically skipping to his car. *Man, he has a nice ass*, was where my mind went. *Who cares about paddleboating if you get to be with him?* I asked myself.

We stored his camera equipment and trudged back to the Basin. I trudged, actually, while Aaron chatted and ran circles around me, prodding me to move faster. There was a short line for the boats. While we waited, we listened to the safety rules and were told we would all be wearing life vests. I turned to look at my companion. Really? He was either ignoring my annoyance or totally entranced by the safety operator's speech. I figured it was the former.

We opted for one without the canopy. It wasn't a warm day, and the canopy was marginally more expensive. We put on our life vests, got on our boat, and began our hour adventure on the paddleboat.

Aaron's reactions to the experience were worth a hundred times the measly twelve bucks we paid. He was in awe of everything.

"Oh my gosh, you can see the mountains from here! Pedal faster, Matty!"

We had a contest to see who could pedal the fastest. I worked up a sweat trying to outdo my companion, who turned out to be an expert paddleboat pedaler. I had to chuckle at his competitive nature. I called a truce when my thighs started to ache. Aaron grinned wildly and threw his arms in the air.

"Woo-hoo! Paddle pedal champion!"

I laughed helplessly at his exuberance. It was catchy. And once again, I was completely charmed.

We let the boat drift aimlessly for a while and just enjoyed the scenery. It truly was a spectacular day. The sun had beat out the clouds, providing a gorgeous backlight to the cherry blossoms' pink blush, the emerald greens of the lawn, and the gray-blue hues of the water and sky above us. Aaron, as usual, talked enough for both of us. He told me this was one of those silly things he'd always wanted to do as a kid, but never got a chance to.

"You ever notice that when people live and work in the same city all their lives, they never visit the so-called tourist traps? I mean, you said so yourself, this is something tourists do, but have you ever done it? I bet there are hundreds if not thousands of people who live in Orlando but have never been to Disney World."

"That could have something to do with the price of admission," I observed, leaning back in my chair and taking in the way the sunlight shone on Aaron's dark hair. Fuck, what a beautiful man.

"True. Alright, maybe that wasn't a good example. Let's see. Well, how about you? What do you want to see or do in DC that you haven't done since you've lived here? You must have a mental checklist. Name something."

"Let me think." I paused, considering what I might want to do that I hadn't yet done in the city. "Well, I guess I have a few. I want to go to a Redskins game. Not because I'm a fan, per se, but...."

"Baseball?"

"No. Football. And I'm pretty sure you knew that." He shrugged innocently, urging me to continue. "Another thing is...." I paused, suddenly feeling a little self-conscious.

"What? Tell me! Come on, you're on a fucking paddleboat with me. Tell me whatever it is, and I'll do it with you!" He threw his head back, closed his eyes, and sent up a mock prayer. "Oh God, please don't make it sports!"

I gave him a weak shove and admitted the one thing I was really interested in seeing was Ford's Theatre.

"You know, where President Lincoln was killed."

"I know. I went there for a field trip when I was in grade school."

"I've never been." I shrugged, feeling a little embarrassed for no real reason.

"Let's go, then! I think we can just show up, but we'll call and see. We can go today!"

I gave him my "you've got to be kidding" look, but he wasn't kidding. And I started thinking, *What the hell? He's right, how easy is it to put off doing things you're interested in because they're almost too accessible? You think you can always do it another time, and then years go by and that box is left unchecked on your To Do list.*

"Today?"

"Why not? It's not even noon. We can leave one of our cars and just go for it. I'm game if you are."

I couldn't offer a good reason not to, so I smiled at him and nodded in agreement.

"Yeah! More adventures!"

We got our full hour's worth of the boat before heading back to the dock. I insisted on taking his picture with my phone to record his first paddleboat jaunt. He posed like a movie star and then asked the employees to take our picture together. I put my arm around him for the picture, knowing this was our first photo together.

Aaron was excited to head out to our next adventure. Once again, I found myself following him, shaking my head at his endless sense of wonder. We chose to take his car to the theater because it was closer. I'd never driven in Aaron's car, and I found I wasn't anxious to be his passenger any time soon. The guy drove like a demon. I was working my phantom foot brake and holding onto the door before we were halfway there.

We purchased tickets for an early afternoon tour and set out to grab lunch at one of Aaron's favorite pizza places close by. He ordered a salad, but kept staring at my pizza longingly. I finally shoved a piece on his plate. He looked surprised and about to refuse, but instead, he gave me one of his spectacular smiles and took a big bite. I watched him closely. He looked like he was performing a sex act, his face a picture of bliss as he licked the cheese from his fingers. When I got caught staring, I gave him a weak shrug. I suddenly wished we'd just gone back to his place. I wanted him. He touched my knee under the table, and we held one another's stare a moment longer. There was a promise in that look. I just needed to be patient.

The Ford's Theatre tour was awesome. I admit to being a bit of a history junkie, and I was on the edge of my seat listening to the sequence of events leading to the murder of our nation's sixteenth president. I was especially interested in seeing the Petersen House across the street, where Lincoln actually died.

I left Ford's Theatre very happy that we'd gone.

"Thanks." I nudged Aaron's elbow in a buddy-like fashion.

"You liked?" He nudged me back and smiled sweetly.

"I did. It's been a fun day of firsts." He nodded in silent agreement. "So, I have one more first to request before we go back to your place for hot sweaty monkey sex."

Aaron took a swift look around us to see if we'd been overheard.

"Shhh! Geez, Matty, this is a respectable tourist neighborhood! Control yourself!" He mock-admonished me with a smack on the arm. "What is your final request? Let's see if this genie will grant your wish."

"Give me your keys, please. There's no fucking way I'm driving with you behind the wheel again. No offense, babe, but you're scary!"

Aaron handed over the keys but insisted the entire ride back to my car that I was bossy and had an inflated opinion of my own driving skills. When we reached my car back at the Tidal Basin, I leaned across the seat and put my hand over his mouth.

"No more talking. Meet you back at your place. Okay?" He nodded. "And Aaron? Thank you. That was fun. Let's go have a different kind of fun now. No clothes required. Okay?" He nodded again. The weekend was only half over and there was so much more to look forward to.

| 9 |

A COUPLE of weeks later, on a Saturday morning, we arranged to meet for a run before heading back to his place to shower and spend the rest of the weekend together. It was raining, which never deterred an avid runner like Aaron. I, however, was really not looking forward to running in the elements. I was a fair-weather runner, but I made the effort to keep my complaints down so Aaron wouldn't uninvite me. I could do it if he could.

We started out at a slow pace and chatted about things we may have missed while apart over the past couple of days. Truthfully we talked or texted many times a day, so it was almost a wonder we found as much to talk about as we did. Aaron picked up the pace and I followed along, although my ability to talk became limited as he chattered on. The sky suddenly darkened to a foreboding shade of gray, threatening to dump some serious precipitation instead of the lighter variety we'd been experiencing. We didn't have to wait long before the first rumbles of thunder sounded. Aaron looked over at me with a maniacally happy grin. The little fucker loved this! The rain fell in torrents, coming down so fast you could barely see in front of you. Lightening flashed, and Aaron laughed out loud as I jumped in fright.

He kept right on running and I kept on following, calling myself all kinds of idiot that I didn't raise the white flag and beg him to show some mercy. We were nowhere near our cars, so our best bet would be to take shelter at a coffee shop until the worst of the storm passed. A mile later, I signaled for him to stop. He didn't. He grinned and kept going. Asshole. I caught up to him and grabbed his arm, forcing him to slow down.

"Please! I'm drowning!" I yelled above the din of thunder.

Aaron rolled his eyes but gamely agreed to stop at the next little coffee shop on our route.

"We are soaked! They don't want us getting their floors wet. Come on, Matty. It's only two more miles back to the cars."

A blast of lightning flashed, sending an eerie glow over the street.

"Fuck that. Come on. And fuck their floors. We should be swimming, not running." I pulled him inside, and we both did our best to shake off the worst of the wet from our clothes and hair before fully entering the shop. It didn't really help, though. We looked like two half-drowned rats. I told Aaron to grab a table, and I ordered us a couple of hot cocoas. Not a fitness beverage, I know, but I needed the comfort. Aaron didn't complain. In fact, he had his best and biggest smile on when I presented him with his drink.

"What are you smiling about? This is miserable!" I shook my sopping-wet hair in his direction, which only made him giggle more. He looked so fucking happy, I found myself returning his smile in spite of being really wet and very uncomfortable.

"It's not miserable. It's fun! This is the best kind of day, Matty! I love it!"

It was on the tip of my tongue to say, "And I love you," but I caught myself. I shook my head and he laughed again, unaware of the inner turmoil I had just set into play. Did I love him? I stopped myself from overthinking the sentiment as I looked across the table at my soaking-wet running partner and reminded myself to live in the moment. I would surely scare him away if I uttered the L-word. Fuck, I was scaring myself! I swiped a finger full of whipped cream from the top of my drink and licked it off suggestively. Aaron's eyes went from amused to sultry in a heartbeat.

"Drink up, honey. We have to run to our rides before we can get home and get naked."

I groaned.

"Can't we call a taxi to take us to our cars?"

"You are whining, naughty boy! And the answer is no. We can do it!"

"Damn right I'm whining. There is nothing on me that isn't wet."

"Ooo, that's sexy."

"Sexy? How? Never mind. I'm ready when you are."

My choice of hot cocoa wasn't the best type of fuel to run on. I had a side cramp a mile into the run and had to stop. Aaron caught sight of me clutching my side and ran back to check on me.

"Want to walk?" His brow was furrowed in concern.

"No, but yes, I have to. Go on. I'll meet you back at your place. No sense in us both being stuck out here longer than necessary." I leaned over at my waist with my hands on my knees, trying to breathe through the worst of the pain.

"Don't be silly. We'll take a slow walk in the rain. So romantic."

I made the effort to look up at him and saw his teasing grin. He was more adorable to me than ever in that moment. The L-word sprang to the tip of my tongue again. I wanted to tell him how good it felt to be with him, even when I was hunched over, clutching my side in pain in the pouring rain. Somehow, in spite of it all, this did feel romantic.

I returned his smile and made a valiant effort to start walking. It was slow going at first, with the rain continuing its incessant tattoo. Aaron kept a steady stream of chatter as we made our way at a leisurely pace. He didn't require much input from me as he set about telling me a story about being stuck in the rain when he was at college, locked out of his dorm. I realized he was setting me at ease in his own way. Attempting to entertain me with a tale he no doubt greatly embellished for entertainment purposes, all to keep my mind off my body's aches and the long walk ahead of us. It worked. I found myself laughing along with him, noting his quick hand movements keeping time with his animated storytelling. The rain had flattened his hair, but he still had to brush it from his eyes every once in a while. I marveled that the simplest of acts made me yearn to touch him.

We were both shivering in earnest by the time we finally reached our cars. Aaron gave me a quick kiss on the lips, telling me he'd see me at home. I heard the word "home" and decided it fit. I followed him and parked directly behind him, grabbing my overnight bag and my guitar case. I don't know what prompted me to bring it, but I wasn't leaving it in my car. He helped me schlep my stuff to the front door. We both let out audible sighs of relief once we were finally inside the building's relatively warm lobby.

His apartment, of course, was fucking freezing. We dropped my belongings at the door and started undressing as fast as possible. Aaron turned on the heater on his way to the bathroom to get the shower going. We had talked about a steaming-hot shower being our reward, and I for one couldn't wait.

Aaron called for me to hurry up. He was already under the spray when I got there, smiling a dreamy, happy smile.

"Hurry! You're frozen, dummy! We need to warm you up. Don't worry, I'll do all the work. Just stand under the water. Let me take care of you."

I did as I was told. The warm water was nirvana. Aaron soaped up his hands and washed me thoroughly. His touch was a magic elixir. So good.

"Bend down so I can wash your hair."

I obeyed wordlessly, reveling in the feel of his fingers massaging my scalp.

"Rinse off, honey."

My body was boneless and beyond exhausted, but I wanted to offer him the same treatment. He gently refused my overture, telling me to get toweled off and in some warm clothes immediately. He sounded like my mom. I told him so, which earned me a smack on my right ass cheek.

"Fine! I'm going! I'm going!"

"Good boy. I'll be right out."

Aaron made us hot tea once he was dressed. I sat on his sofa, finally feeling the warmth from the heater as well as my comfortable dry clothing. I picked my guitar up out of its case and strummed a few chords, making sure it was still in key.

"I love that you brought your guitar! What will you play for me?" Aaron looked delicious in a pair of flannel pj's and a tight-fitting long-sleeved T-shirt. His hair was a little mussed from the shower, and I was hoping he'd leave it that way. He looked boyishly adorable.

"I don't know why I brought it, honestly. Total impulse, I guess." I was a little self-conscious.

"Don't be shy! I've heard you play, remember? I know you're good. Play me a song, Matty."

I started to play an Elton John song. The original version was played on the piano, but I'd been working on the guitar adaptation.

"Pretty. What is it?"

"'Your Song'. It's by Elton John. You know it?"

"No. What are the words?"

I was going to say I couldn't believe he didn't know that song, but really, why would he? He liked techno-pop dance music. Plus this was an older song. Maybe he'd heard it when he was a kid but didn't recall.

I started from the top and sang softly to him. The words were a perfect sentiment to how I felt about him. I couldn't say the words, but I hoped he would get the message through the music.

"It's a little bit funny, this feeling inside...."

I didn't look at him until I finished the last line.

He had a tear in his eye. He did understand.

I set my guitar aside, reached for him, and pulled him close to me. I just wanted to hold him, smell him, feel him. Yeah, "this feeling inside." Whatever it was, it felt pretty fucking powerful.

| 10 |

ONE thing about being with Aaron that I couldn't deny was the sex was the best I'd ever had, bar none. Everything felt new and exciting. I knew Aaron had plenty of experience, but he made me feel as though everything we did in bed was earth-shattering to him as well. The more I got to know him, the more I realized he wasn't one to placate feelings. He was very straightforward and sure of himself. He knew what he wanted and wasn't afraid to use his sexy self to get it. And the one thing Aaron really liked was sex. It wasn't unusual to wake up on a Sunday morning with him nudging his ass back against my groin in invitation. I couldn't believe how fast or how hard I became just from the press of his backside against my cock.

I woke up one such Sunday with his ass wiggling insistently for attention. He knew I was awake and had taken the liberty of preparing himself for me while I worked to get a condom on my achingly hard dick. Aaron lifted his right leg for easier access as I slowly made my way inside. He was so tight and perfect. His reactions alone could throw me into a sexual frenzy. The way he responded to me was intoxicating and powerful. I couldn't get enough of him. I draped my right leg over him, covering his body as

I rolled him onto his stomach. He let me fuck him while lying flat, but then he shifted his ass back toward me so he could get his knees under him. I loved being behind him like that. It was so primal, and it was invariably the position that had him screaming for more and "fuck me, Matty, do it" over and over. I came in a huge rush, like I was literally falling apart. I rested my forehead on Aaron's back for a second and then reached around to stroke him as he rode his orgasm out on my cock, pouring himself into my hand.

We both fell boneless onto the mattress, panting. I kissed his neck and gently eased myself from his ass. He flinched and I shot him a look when I got up to get rid of the condom.

"Matty, I'm fine. Fuck, that was crazy good." He rolled to his side and then started when he hit the wet spot. "Yuck."

"Time to change the sheets, babe. I'll help you," I suggested as I handed him a warm washcloth.

"Actually, I was thinking…."

"Uh-oh."

"Quiet, peanut gallery," he said, smacking my arm. "Let's go shopping."

"Um…."

"I know, I know. You hate it, but I promise to be quick! I need a new set of sheets at the rate we're wearing them out, plus I have to get a birthday gift for my mom." He batted his eyelashes at me. What was I supposed to say?

An hour and a half later, I found myself in my own personal version of hell… a department store catering to household goods and women's wear. Ugh!

Sheets were easy. Aaron was very specific about thread count (700-plus only), color (charcoal), and brand (whatever it was, it was pricey). We were in and out of the bedding and linens section within fifteen minutes. The women's department was another story. It was teeming with females, young, old, and everywhere in between, and the occasional sorry-looking husband or boyfriend trailing miserably behind them.

For the first time it struck me that I was still in the category of the miserable schmuck following his partner around in the mall, but my "partner" was a guy, not a girl. Aaron wasn't just a friend I was accompanying to the mall. I had done this before, but with girlfriends. Aaron and I had done a lot of other things I'd done with women too. We'd gone to the movies, dinner, running, and the gym. Why did this feel different? I had a sudden moment of clarity that it was because I was doing something I didn't really want to do to please Aaron. Not just to please him, though, but also because I wanted to be with him more than I didn't want to be sniffing fragrances at the perfume counter on a Sunday morning.

Sure, we'd gone running in the rain and I hadn't liked that, but that was physical exercise. I would be a wimp to not go with him. This was different. This going to the mall business reminded me of being a little boy trailing behind my mom, begging to go home. Invariably my siblings and I would fight, my mom would be angry with us, and chances were we'd be punished for being total brats. Not fun.

A wave of panic filled me. I felt suddenly sick to my stomach and out of sorts. I wanted out. Out of this overcrowded, overly warm department store. I looked for Aaron, who was busily chatting with a pretty young salesgirl about the nuances of a fruity versus musky scent. He didn't seem to notice my internal freak-out session. The young girl was flirting with him, and he went right along with it, asking her opinion and charming her in general, the way he always seemed to do. Waiters, shop owners, bartenders... they all loved him. His affable, sweet manner and silly sense of humor drew people to him. I focused on him and could feel myself begin to relax. I was where I wanted to be. I was with Aaron, and for some inexplicable reason, he wanted to be with me too. Deep breath.

"Matt?"

I gave a start and turned away from Aaron and his new best friend, the perfume girl, to find Kristin standing at the counter behind me. She gave me a hesitant smile. We hadn't seen one another in a couple months. It was obvious neither of us knew how to approach the other. This could be awkward.

"Hi. How are you?" That seemed safe enough.

"Good, good. What are you doing in a mall? You hate shopping."

"I'm waiting for a friend." A friend. Shit. This was about to get really awkward. I glanced nervously in Aaron's direction, wondering how to handle this. Was this a coming-out moment? I felt that wave racing toward me, and my earlier bout of panic returned full force.

Kristin followed my gaze and gave me a sad smile. I caught on almost immediately that she assumed I was with Ms. Perfume, maybe waiting for her to finish work. This was a chance to dispel that theory. Was I brave enough? Was I ready?

"Hey, honey! There you are. I'm ready. I think I found one she'll like." Aaron put his hand on my arm as he was jostled by a hurried shopper.

Those surreal moments happen to everyone at some point in life. The ones where two worlds collide and no one is sure of how to react. This was certainly one of those bizarre events. Past girlfriend, current boyfriend (although neither of us had used the term yet), and the guy who knows them both but has no fucking idea how to introduce one to the other. Hence, he wishes himself anywhere but where he currently finds himself.

"Hi, I'm Aaron." Aaron obviously had decided the uncomfortable silence had gone on a minute too long. He looked between the two of us as if for clues to the strange exchange we were all engaged in.

"Sorry. Aaron, this is Kristin." My voice sounded weak to my own ears.

"Hi, Kristin! I just dragged Matt with me to find a gift. Sunday at the mall. So not his favorite."

Was it my imagination, or had Aaron just turned into a girl? He had turned on his effeminate side full force. Awkward had gone to downright uncomfortable. He was projecting a "don't mind me, I'm just his queer friend" vibe. It was strange and unsuited to who we had become.

"I remember," Kristin replied weakly. "I'll let you go. Nice to see you, Matt."

I stared after her for no other reason than I didn't know how to deal with Aaron, who stood beside me, ominously silent. What had happened here? More than a chance meeting with an ex who appeared to not quite be over "us" while with the man I was currently seeing. This was about me not addressing a significant change in my life. At that particular moment, however, it was more than I could deal with at all.

Aaron didn't say a word as we left the congested department store and headed out toward the parking lot, I was quiet too. I needed a little space and time to process what had just occurred. I followed him up to his place and gathered my belongings while he unpacked his purchases. We made small talk about his mom's birthday, but we both seemed a little relieved when I made my way to the front door. Or maybe that was just me.

"I'll call you." That sounded lame, but I wasn't in the frame of mind to correct myself or explain my confused state of mind.

"Alrighty. Bye, Matty."

Aaron stood on his toes and kissed my cheek. His eyes looked a little sad and watery. I should have said something to get the balance back. I could have made a joke about adventures at the mall and how I'd warned him I was a terrible shopper. But I said nothing. The absence of laughter, teasing, and touching was felt, and the air was heavy with unspoken questions and grievances. I leaned down to kiss his cheek in return and made my escape.

I spent the rest of that day burying my head in law books. When I emerged from my room that night, Curt, Dave, and Jason were sitting around a pizza, taking turns playing killing games on the Xbox. I grabbed a beer and plopped myself in the ratty old armchair. Someone offered me the controls at some point and I took over. The stupid game did more to agitate me than seeing Kristin and pondering my relationship with Aaron had earlier. I lost badly to Dave and chucked the control angrily at the chair, yelling, "Fuck it," as I stormed out of the living room.

I heard my friends asking each other what the hell was my problem. And that certainly was a good question. What the hell was my problem? Was this the big freak-out Aaron had asked about a couple of months ago? A delayed reaction of sorts. I owed him an apology. I'd call him tomorrow, I decided. I needed to do a little soul-searching first.

There was a soft knock on my bedroom door, and Curt peeked his head in a second later.

"Not going to wait to be invited in?" I asked sarcastically.

"No, in the mood you're in, I doubt you would grant me entry. What's up? Girl trouble? Guy trouble?"

I moved some textbooks out of the way and leaned back against my headboard, staring up at the ceiling while trying to gather my thoughts. Curt was the perfect confidante, but I was reluctant to share. He sat in my desk chair and pulled it closer to the bed so he could put his feet up.

"Comfortable?" I sounded like a sullen kid.

"Yep. Now, spill it. I'm a patient guy until you mess with my Xbox, asshole. What's going on with you?"

"Sorry about that. I hate losing to Dave."

"And Jason and me. You hate losing, period, but you don't usually throw shit. Did you have a fight?"

I sighed heavily and finally looked Curt in the eye. Talking to him would help.

"No. Two things happened. The mall, and we bumped into Kristin." I raised an eyebrow, hoping he could infer everything from that tiny bit of info. He didn't disappoint.

"So, first of all, what the fuck were you doing in the mall? It's not Christmas Eve. Must have been talked into it. That would be the small head leading you, I bet. Then you ran into Kristin while in the company of your new 'friend'." He air quoted. "You were flustered because you were in unfriendly territory, aka The Mall, and you freaked when past ran into present. Am I right?"

"Fuck. You are good. Yes, that's exactly it. I freaked. I'm embarrassed to admit it, but I didn't know what to do. I just froze. It was uncomfortable and weird. Aaron is probably pissed too."

"Why? Did you pretend you didn't know him or something?"

"No, but I didn't go out of my way to introduce him as my boyfriend or significant person either. He knows her name, he knows who she is, but... ugh! I froze, I freaked. Aaron asked me if I would do this. I thought I was cool with everything, but I don't know."

"Hold on. Dude, give yourself a break. This is the first time you've been in a 'relationship'"—I rolled my eyes at his air quotes this time—"with a guy. No one is comfy cozy when ex and current meet. This would be no different if you had been with a girl and ran into Kristin."

"Maybe. But it is different, right? Because we're two guys, I feel like I need to explain. Not for Kristin's sake, but for Aaron's. I mean, shouldn't I be wearing a rainbow shirt and introducing him as my boyfriend with a big fucking smile on my face? He deserves more than people assuming that we're just friends. I really like him. If he were a girl, I wouldn't hesitate to put my arm around him and introduce him. I mean, I'm not ashamed. I just don't know how to go forward." I paused and looked over at Curt, willing him to understand. "Does that even make sense?"

"Yeah, it does. And like it or not, it's a baby step in 'coming out'. You've never had a boyfriend, Matt. But seriously, is it really that different than dating a girl? I mean, sex aside, and I'm not going there." He shivered dramatically for effect. "I'm referring to respect. You're with someone romantically, you acknowledge them. Simple, right?"

"We haven't exactly had the old let's be boyfriends talk yet. We just said we'd take it slow. I think that was Aaron realizing I'd fuck up, so let's not get too serious."

"You're turning into a drama queen."

"Fuck off."

"Seriously, talk to him. Tell him you freaked. Ask him about being 'boyfriends'. Assure him that seeing Kristin was just weird and you aren't wishing you were back together. Make sure he knows you want to continue being a big fat homo with him."

I threw a pillow at him, which he neatly dodged.

"You make it sound so simple."

"I just think it's normal to freak. Aaron sounds like a cool guy. He must be, if you're willing to engage in hot kinky man sex with him."

I gave him my best dirty look.

"No details? Fine. Whatever. My point is gay relationships are the same as straight ones. Communicate. You don't communicate and it all goes to shit."

Curt stood up to leave.

"Thanks."

"No problem, man. But if you throw my controllers again, I'll have to kill you."

I took a deep breath. Curt was right. I'd call Aaron tomorrow to talk.

| 11 |

I SENT Aaron a "good morning" text first thing Monday before heading off to class. I had a full day ahead of me, and I was hoping we could meet later that night. Aaron usually returned text messages immediately. His phone was practically glued to his hand. The guy was a social media enthusiast. When I didn't receive a text from him by noon, I began to worry. Unfortunately, I was due at the law office and didn't have a chance to do more than send a second message. By late afternoon, when neither text was returned, I had a feeling something was up. I called his cell, but it went straight to voice mail. Not good.

I got a little obnoxious and started leaving messages every hour.

"Aaron, hi. Call me when you get a chance. I was hoping we could maybe go have dinner tonight. You free?"

"Hi again. I haven't heard back from you. Busy day? Call me when you get a minute."

"Where are you? Did you have a good day? Call me. I want to talk to you."

"Baby, please. You're mad, aren't you? Call me."

"Aaron, please. Call me."

I had to talk myself out of going to his apartment. A ton of messages and texts should get the message across. If he didn't call me in the morning, though, all bets were off.

I sent him a text first thing the next morning. Again, no response. At noon, I sent a very long text.

Ok ur mad.

U must b. I'm sorry. Plz call me.

We nd to talk. R u home tonite?

I want 2come over

Please

Nothing. Nada. Zilch. I was getting mad. I hated the silent treatment. Really hated it. If you're pissed off at me, be pissed off. But don't ignore me, damn it. My anger turned to concern when I realized I hadn't heard anything from him in forty-eight hours. I checked online to see if he'd posted anything, but it looked like he had gone radio silent there also. I called again, left yet another pathetic "please call me" message before getting in my car and heading over to his place.

His BMW was parked on the street in front of his building, so I figured he was home. Or wait, maybe he went out. I drove when we went out because he hated to lose a prime parking spot, plus he hated driving, and in my opinion was a menace on the roads. Did he have a date? Was there someone else? We hadn't said we were exclusive. We'd never said we were committed. The word "boyfriend" never was mentioned. We were going slow. Aaron wanted it that way. Fuck! My errant head was a mess in more ways than one. Jealousy was eating a hole in my stomach with just the thought of him with someone else.

I decided not to call or text that I was out front. I was sure I would keep getting the silent treatment. A sneak attack was called for. I waited until I saw another tenant enter the main door and slipped in with her. Making my way to his floor, I said a brief prayer that he would (a) talk to me, and (b) be alone. I had worked myself into a cool sweat by the time I actually knocked on his door. There was no music blaring from inside, so I figured he heard my knock. I tried again, louder this time. I became concerned that no music was a bad thing. Desperate now, I started thinking he was hurt. Maybe he wasn't answering because he couldn't. I banged on the door and yelled for him to open it.

"Aaron! It's me. Please open the door. You are freaking me out. You haven't returned my calls or messages for two fucking d…."

The door opened abruptly and an irate-looking Aaron was impatiently waving me in.

"For fuck's sake! Would you keep it down! Jesus, Matt. The neighbors will be calling the police. Come in already!"

I breathed a sigh of relief as I stepped into his apartment. He was fine. I quickly switched to anger. That meant I was being ignored. What the fuck?

"Why have you been avoiding me? You haven't responded to my texts, calls. I went from irritated to concerned to fucking frantic over forty-eight fucking hours. Geez." I paced while I blasted him. I had all this crazy energy now. The man was making me nuts.

He stood in his entryway with his arms folded, giving me an appraising stare. He must have just returned from work. He was wearing a pair of tight-fitting khaki dress pants with a blue-and-white striped oxford shirt. Gorgeous. I wanted to reach out, grab him, touch him, brush his hair away from his eyes, run my hands over his ass. None of that was going to happen, according to his body language. Something was up. I'd been given the silent treatment for a reason, and it seemed as though I was finally going to find out why.

"So, you're telling me that you were banging on my door like a man possessed because you were worried about me? What were you going to do? Break the damn door down? Calm yourself, He-Man. I'm fine."

"How the hell would I know that? You have been ignoring me for days!" I was trying not to lose my cool, but he was frustrating, to say the least.

Aaron let out a long, tired sigh, unfolded his arms, and walked into his kitchen.

"Want anything to drink?" He grabbed a water bottle and tossed one to me before I could answer.

"Thanks." I followed him back into his living room and sat on the opposite end of the sofa. My hands were clammy. I had a sinking sensation I wasn't going to like whatever he had to say. His posture was rigid and tense. He wasn't happy.

"Matt. I can't do this." He held up a hand to stop me from speaking. "I had a feeling that the straight guy turned gay was a bad idea for me, and I was right."

"Aaron, you're being dramatic. Why is this a bad idea? Everything about this, me and you, is good."

He shook his head. He looked tired and resigned. Neither were good signs for me.

"Look, I said we'd go slow and see how we feel. The other day, Matt... you looked so miserable being with me. And when we ran into your ex. Ugh. First of all, you never told me how beautiful she was or that she was head over heels in love with you. Did you even notice how she looked at you? No. I bet not. I'm not sure what you told her before you introduced us, but it certainly wasn't, 'Hey, that's the guy I'm sleeping with.' Not that I expected it, but fuck! You looked so unhappy, so trapped. It was everything I was afraid of." He paused, visibly upset. "Matt, I'm gay. I'm out, I'm proud. I don't know how to be anything or anyone else. I never have. My dad has been lamenting the fact for years now, hoping I'll grow out of it and bring home a nice Catholic girl. It will never happen. For you, it could happen."

"I'm not Catholic," I said lamely.

"Matt, I'm not sure you know who you are or what you want. We are good together. We have fun. I love being with you. I won't lie. But my problem is that I'm becoming a little too attached to someone with too much baggage. I told you I like to travel lightly."

"You aren't making any sense." I stood up to pace again. I was too agitated to sit still. "I'm sorry I freaked out. You're right. I had a moment where I realized I didn't want to be at the fucking mall because I hate the fucking mall, but there I was. With you. Because I wanted to be with you more than I didn't want to be there. And yeah, it scared me. It felt couple-y." He shot me a frustrated look. "But I liked it, Aaron. I... we just hadn't talked about any of it. And then, out of the blue, there's Kristin! I'm sorry I didn't tell her you were special to me. I was tongue-tied and stupid and I'm sorry. I freaked."

Silence. I waited for him to speak. I had apologized, so I figured the ball was in his court. I sat back down.

"I can't take a chance, Matt. I'm sorry too."

"What do you mean? Aar, please. What do you want me to do? I... I want you, I want us. I'm in virgin territory here, babe. Do you want me to publicly announce I'm dating a man? Which opens a whole other set of questions for me. Are we dating? Just lovers? What do you want from us?"

"Nothing, Matt."

"Aar, you can't mean that. I'm sorry for Sunday. A million times over. Please."

"Don't you get it? It isn't just about Sunday! Matt, you say you want us, but come on! You looked visibly sick when you ran into your ex. I think you need some space to figure out what you want in your future. I'm the first guy you've ever been with. I don't want to think this hasn't meant anything to you, but maybe you need something more familiar."

"What? Kristin? I don't want her. I don't want a different girl, nor do I want to experiment with other guys. I've been with another guy before. I want you, Aaron. Only you."

He let out a deep breath and turned to face me. There was a tear on his eyelash.

"I won't settle anymore. I get that life doesn't come with guarantees, but I want something that looks like it could be the real thing. I don't want to be someone's dirty secret. I want the man I'm with to be proud to be with me. You can't give me what I need, Matt. I don't think it's because you don't want to. I just don't think you're ready."

Tears were rolling down his face in earnest now. I leapt to his side to comfort him, to tell him he was being crazy, to fight for my cause. He put his arm up to shield my advance and shot to his feet.

"Please go, Matt." He turned, walked to the front door, and held it open for me to leave.

My heart was in my throat. I didn't know what to say. He was breaking my heart. So I told him the truth.

"Aaron. I love you."

His head snapped up.

"Matt...."

"I do, Aaron. I've never felt this way about anyone. I know."

I probably sounded a little manic. It was how I felt. Crazy. And yet somehow sure that I was absolutely telling the truth.

He didn't look convinced. In fact, he seemed upset.

"Matt, go. You don't know what you're saying. Please, just go."

The look on his face was heart wrenching, and it killed me to know I had something to do with putting it there.

"Look, I'll go now, but Aaron... I'm serious, and somehow, some way I'll prove it to you. You... matter. This matters."

I kissed him quickly on the cheek and left before I could say anything else. I needed to retreat and figure out how to convince him that what I said was true. I was in love with him.

EASIER said than done. Aaron wouldn't accept my phone calls, and stalking him was just plain creepy. I decided to enlist Curt's help. His advice hadn't exactly worked for me yet, but it was sound nonetheless. And at this point, it certainly couldn't hurt.

"What you need to do is wow him."

"Huh? How?"

We were at a dive bar near our apartment. I didn't want to go into the whole story when Dave got back from work, so I asked Curt to meet me for a beer.

"Matt, you are so dense sometimes. What does your instinct tell you to do? You know him better than me. Christ! What does he like to do? Where does he like to go? Suppose we were talking about a girl, what would you do?"

"We aren't talking about a girl, asshole. Geez, he likes to dance, he likes to run, he loves romantic movies with happy endings, he's a great cook, he loves his friends, his family.... How does any of this help me?"

"Well, I don't know exactly, but maybe it would be a good idea to enlist his best friend to help your cause. He might be able to help make something happen, or encourage him to listen to you. Do you think he would?"

"I don't know. I guess it's worth a shot. Aaron's giving me the silent treatment." I took a long swig of my beer before I continued.

"Curt, I'm a fucking mess. He's all I can think about. I can't sleep, I can barely concentrate at school and work. Shit! I don't know what's wrong with me."

"Love?" He looked at me like he knew I would pounce on that one little word and kick his ass for even mentioning it. When I didn't, his eyebrows shot comically up to his hairline. "You're in love?"

I shrugged. Yeah, and it was definitely not all hearts and roses, if my current sad-sack condition was any evidence.

"Well, if that's the case, man, make it big. Who's his best friend? Maybe he'll help you out."

The thing was, I wasn't sure Jay would help me. My guess was he would protect Aaron from me, assuming I would unintentionally hurt him. Peter, on the other hand, might help me get to him through Jay. It was worth a try.

GETTING in touch with Peter would be the tricky part. I knew the firm he worked for, but little else. If they asked any questions about departments or gave me a chain of voice mails, I could be screwed. I placed a call the following morning in between classes. The number was a general one, which thankfully led me to Peter Morgan's secretary in just four call transfers. She was very polite, told me Mr. Morgan was currently out of the office, but she would leave him a message. I didn't want to risk that Peter wouldn't know who I was, especially since I was contacting him at work and this was personal. I asked for his direct voice mail when she told me she couldn't give out his private cell phone number. When I hung up, I felt pretty good. Hell, it was better than nothing.

I had a message waiting for me when I got out of class. It was Peter.

"Hi, Matt. Peter returning your call. Give me a call."

The tone of the message was businesslike, but the fact he returned my call at all seemed like a positive. Whatever. I couldn't afford to waste time overthinking. I called him back immediately.

"Peter Morgan" came the brisk reply on the first ring.

"Hi, Peter. This is Matt Sullivan. Thanks for calling back."

"Hey, Matt. What can I do for you?"

"Um, well, this is a little awkward...." I really hadn't thought how to phrase my request.

"It's Aaron, right?"

"Yeah, I...."

"I can't really talk at the moment, but why don't you meet me at the Old Regent for a drink at five. You free?"

"Yes, I'll be there."

"Great. See you then."

Step one accomplished. Now I had to figure out how to get him to help me.

I ARRIVED at the Old Regent ten minutes early and found a seat at a high table for two. It would give us a little privacy, which was a bonus. The bar Peter had chosen was very high-end and catered to well-known politicians and lobbyists. I was glad I'd come from work so I was at least dressed for the upscale atmosphere. The heavy oak paneling and crystal chandeliers were old-money posh. Elaborate floral arrangements told me I wasn't in a "normal" bar. My usual student attire would have made me feel out of place amongst the super elite DC after-work crowd. I needed a boost to my confidence, no matter how shallow the means.

I had just ordered a vodka martini when I caught sight of Peter with his phone pressed to his ear, pacing just outside the entrance. He spotted me and held up a hand in greeting, also indicating he might be stuck on the phone a bit longer. I nodded in response. Peter was every bit the well-heeled businessman in his expensively tailored suit and elegant air. The guy had most likely just put in a ten-plus-hour day even though it was only 5:00 p.m., but he still looked sharp. The sexy afternoon stubble didn't hurt matters either. The man was stunning. Gay or straight, it couldn't be denied.

"Sorry about that. Client." He shook my hand and signaled to the waiter with the other.

"No problem. Thank you for meeting me."

"So... Aaron?"

"Yeah. How did you guess?"

Peter's eyes twinkled with amusement and a wry smile.

"Jay is my partner. Aaron is his best friend. Those two are like... well, never mind. Let's just say, Jay and I have been together for a few years now, so I know that if something is bothering one of them, the other will know all about it."

"So you already know?"

"I try not to pay too much attention, but either way, what is it I can help you with?"

In other words, man up, cards on the table, Matt. I took a deep breath and asked for help.

"What do you want me to do, exactly?" He hadn't refused, which was good, but I didn't know what I wanted him to do, exactly.

"I need to convince him somehow, right? You just told me how tight he and Jay are. Can you persuade Jay to convince Aaron to at least hear me out?"

"Maybe. Jay isn't exactly a pushover. He won't help just because I ask if he's truly concerned you're a danger to Aaron. I mean emotionally, of course. He'll help if he thinks it's in Aaron's best interest, but honestly, Matt, I'm not sure how to play that one. I've been with women too, and I understand that sexuality isn't cut and dry. Aaron and Jay aren't as giving on the idea. I think Aaron is afraid of being an experiment to you. So this is a tough one."

"I get that, but it's not true. I... I tried to tell him. I've never felt this way about anyone. Any girl, any guy... this is different. I won't change my mind."

We were both silent for a few minutes. A piano man sat at the baby grand in the corner of the bar and ran his hands over the keys, warming up to perform for the after-work crowd. Inspiration struck like a bolt out of the blue. I knew exactly what I needed to do, but I still needed Peter's help.

We discussed my plan over a second cocktail before shaking hands and parting ways. For the first time in days, I had a feeling I could win Aaron back. I practically skipped to my car. Things were looking up.

| 12 |

OF COURSE, nothing was ever easy. Peter sent me a text message, having to delay my plan due to work travel. I couldn't really fault his priorities, but I was anxious. Each day that went by, my initial excitement wore thin. I was beginning to despair. And people were beginning to notice. My roommates gave me a wide berth and exchanged bewildered looks. I hadn't shared anything more with Curt, and I think he was losing patience with my moodiness. Finally, Dave confronted me.

"I'm staging an intervention. What the fuck is your problem? You've been like a chick on her period for weeks! Did you break up with your mystery girlfriend? Fail a class? Something at work? What is it?"

Jason was over too. He had come be to watch a baseball game with the guys. Beer bottles were already littering our ancient, stained coffee table. I had had a beer with them and was about to retire to my room to study when Dave called me out. He was right. I was moody and out of sorts. It wasn't a wonder they would notice. Curt hadn't said anything to them, and he didn't know anything new. I'm sure he was equally curious about what the fuck was up with me.

I turned back to join them in the living room. It was confession time. I couldn't take the duplicity or lies of omission any longer. If they were disgusted or couldn't understand, I'd just have to deal with the fallout.

"I apologize for being an ass. I've been distracted." I swiped my hand through my hair distractedly.

"Yeah, dickhead. We get that. What's the prob?"

"I met someone who means a lot to me, and things got complicated. I'm trying to work it out but it isn't going well." Shit, I still sounded evasive even to my own ears. I shrugged and started picking at the label on my empty beer bottle.

"Erin? Isn't that her name? We haven't even met her. Did she dump you or something?"

"Yeah. But it's Aaron with an A."

Dave and Jason just stared at me with matching blank expressions, most likely puzzled as to why I would think they would care even remotely how a girl spelled her name. Curt, however, sputtered his beer and was busy choking. He got what I was doing.

"Aaron is a guy."

The baseball announcer's voice, excitedly reporting a line drive to third, was the only sound in the room. Dave and Jason wore incredulous expressions, and Curt looked pretty damned surprised. Guess he didn't think I had it in me.

I had wondered how it would go down... this big reveal. Would it be met with congratulations and have its own soundtrack playing in the background? Some song from the disco era claiming me as a new and welcome member of the gay community? Maybe that Gloria Gaynor song. All the gay men I knew, including Curt, loved that song. "I Will Survive." Rather fitting, actually.

Reality wasn't so rainbow colored. In fact, it was kind of anticlimactic. No soundtrack, just the sounds of baseball on the television mixed with an increasingly uncomfortable quiet. I waited a minute or two longer before the silence threatened to unnerve me.

"Well? Aren't you going to say anything?"

"Uh, yeah... are you punkin' us? What's going on?" Dave asked once he found his voice.

"No, I'm serious. You guys actually did meet him, but it's been a while. I met him at Club Indigo last year." Their faces were blank. Probably still in shock, I guessed. "The four of us went dancing. We went with Curt. Look, it doesn't matter. You wouldn't remember. We didn't start seeing each other anyway until earlier this year after I broke up with Kristin."

More silence.

"Guys... I know this is weird, but I'm still me. Nothing's changed other than Aaron won't fucking return my calls. But me? I'm still Matt."

More silence. Curt finally took pity on me and spoke up.

"We know you're still you, Matt. You guys good?"

"Fuck. Well, yeah. Sure. I'm just fucking shocked. Surprised." Dave shook his head, as though literally trying to wrap his head around a new concept.

"Yeah, man. But, I don't really get it. You've only dated girls the whole time we've known you. Are you just going through a phase, like bi-curious or whatever they call it? You know, something you want to try so you can say 'been there, done that'? Don't get me wrong, I have no problem with gays. We hang out with this loser." Jason slung a friendly arm over Curt's shoulder and mussed his hair.

"I know it may seem weird. And no, I haven't ever dated a guy before. I just think I found the right person, and in my case, it turned out to be a guy, not a girl."

"So, you're gay for him?" Dave looked proud of himself, like maybe he was showing some sign of hipness.

"No, well, maybe. I've always been this way. I'm bi, if we have to put a label out there. I've been attracted to men in the past, but I've also been attracted to women. Because I found women attractive, I just stayed the course there. It was easier. Expected. And I never met a guy I wanted to be with badly enough. Not until I met Aaron."

"So, what happened? He broke up with you? Were you boyfriends?" Dave asked.

"We weren't boyfriends exactly. I mean, we never said that's what we were, but I... I don't know how to explain it. I just fell for him and then I freaked about feeling that way about a man. He couldn't deal with the freak-out."

Dave and Jason nodded sympathetically. I don't think they knew how to respond, but it was nice that they were trying.

"Matt's trying to convince Aaron that he's over the freak session and wants to be with him. Which is probably why he's been a bear to live with recently. Am I right, Matt?" Curt asked in that overly perceptive way of his.

"Yeah. Basically that's it in a nutshell. I have a game plan, but I'm waiting for my reinforcement to get back in town."

I briefed them on my strategy. Curt smiled broadly while Dave and Jason nodded slowly in agreement.

"We'll help too. What do you want us to do?" Dave asked. I would have fallen out of my chair, had I been sitting.

"Thanks for offering, man. I totally appreciate it, but I think it's something I need to do alone."

"Well, good luck, then. Bring him around sometime. Or are you embarrassed of Curt here?" Dave asked, tossing a pillow at Curt's head.

"If he agrees to see me again, then yes, I will. He's cool. Kinda quirky but funny, you know? I think you'd like him if you gave him a chance. He doesn't like sports or hanging out drinking beers all afternoon. But he's great." I was rambling. A glance at my buddies told me so.

"Dude. You are gone. Who cares if he likes sports? Not everyone does. Chelsea doesn't." Jason looked uncomfortable before asking, "Does Kristin know? I'm just curious. Who does know?"

"You guys. No one else. I'm good to go public now, though. It may persuade him that I'm serious. Kristin never knew because there wasn't a reason to say anything. Although we ran into her at the mall and I messed up a great opportunity to, you know...."

"'Come out'," Curt supplied, complete with air quotes.

"Yeah. My head wasn't in the right place. I'm ready now, though."

"Cool." They looked sincere. The relief was intense.

"Thanks, you guys. This means a lot to me."

"Yeah, yeah. Stop being such a dick, though, would you? Get your man back and be normal again. That's all we're asking. Oh... and Matt?"

"Hmm?"

"Bring us another round?" Dave held up his empty beer bottle.

I was a lucky guy, I thought to myself. My friends were solid guys. I was more than a little relieved they were so cool with everything. I gave them a wide smile of appreciation, then flipped Dave the bird before heading to the fridge for more beer.

I HAD played some gigs with my guitar buddy, Sam, over the last couple of Saturdays since Aaron had called us quits. It was something to do that I enjoyed, and it kept me from going bananas.

Plus, it was part of my plan. I was just awaiting Peter's confirmation that Jay was going to help.

One Saturday afternoon, a couple weeks after I'd met up with Peter, I received a call from a John Reynolds. I had no idea who the hell it was, but I took the call, thinking it had something to do with the bar we were scheduled to play at that evening.

"Hi, is this Matt?" The voice had a soft Southern lilt and was familiar, but I couldn't place it right away.

"Yes. Who's this?"

"It's Jay, Matt. Can you talk?"

Fuck yes. Of course I could talk. My heart was beating out of my chest all of a sudden. Finally! Here was the guy I needed to win over to get to Aaron.

"Yes, of course. How are you?" I replied with more calm than I felt.

"I'm fine. Look, I know you talked to Peter about me maybe smoothin' the way with Aaron. I'm being honest when I say I didn't want anything to do with it. I told my man that."

My heart sunk. Why was he calling me, then? To tell me to back off?

"So you won't talk to him?"

"I talk to him all the time! I didn't want anything to do with you and Aaron getting together in whatever capacity you were together as… boyfriends, fuck buddies… whatever, for one reason only. He's my best friend, and I don't want him hurt."

"Okay, but?" There was something he wasn't saying or was just taking a long time to say. I needed him to fucking spit it out.

"I changed my mind."

"That's good." I let out a breath I was aware I'd been holding. "Can I ask what made you change your mind?"

"He's been a tragic mess for the past few weeks. Totally sad and depressed. I'm sure I don't need to tell you, that is so not Aaron. Aaron doesn't do sad. If he does, because I suppose we all have our moments, it never lasts long with him. I hope you aren't upset, but he told me about your declaration of love. For what it's worth, whether it's love or not, Aaron needs to talk to you. I don't want him walking away because he's afraid. If it's love or even the idea that it could be love… well, it is scary. Love is scary. And it's a fucking leap. Excuse my French. So, yes, I will aid and abet. However, I have something to say, and I will say this only one time. You listenin'?"

"Yes?"

"You seem like a genuine guy, and I do like you, Matt. Peter likes you too, and he's much pickier than me. But here's the deal… you hurt him and I will kick your ass. Clear? I'm not some prissy faggot. Don't get on my bad side. Don't mess with him if your heart isn't in the right place."

Jay's voice had gone steely with resolve. I knew he was serious, which I found I appreciated. Aaron was fortunate to have a loyal friend like Jay. Even if he had just threatened me with bodily harm.

"I got it. Jay, thank you. I really miss him. I want to—"

"Yeah, yeah. You don't have to give me details… Aaron will either way. Just make him happy. Please? I think he feels all those things about you too. He's afraid. Fix this, Matt."

"I will, Jay. I will."

We discussed putting my plan into action. Jay reminded me how stubborn Aaron could be and that he almost needed to be convinced the idea was his all along. I wasn't sure how he would react. I was scared he'd walk away and be more pissed than ever, but I had to do something. My greatest fear was that Aaron would eventually convince himself we really were no good for each other. I might not get another chance.

SAM and I were scheduled to play at a small bar in Georgetown called the Whistler later that same evening. Sam was a regular there, playing once a month, which meant he had a modest but loyal fan base. The audience there was a mellow collegiate one, and usually included a few younger teachers. Sam was the guy they were coming to see. I just played a few songs with him, or if he needed a break entirely, I did a couple on my own. Tonight I needed to do one on my own. And most importantly, I needed to time it correctly.

Sam and I went on stage together at 10:00 p.m. and performed a few songs. I took a break, which allowed Sam to show off for his fans, take requests, and do his mini rock star thing. I slipped off to a darkened section of the bar closest to the stage. I could grab a much-needed alcoholic beverage to calm my growing nerves, be close to the stage, and keep an eye on the door all at the same time from this prime location. My hands were a little shaky as I sipped on a vodka tonic. I was fine while I was playing, but the waiting was making me a wreck.

I spotted Aaron the minute he walked through the door. His gorgeous hair was a touch longer than when I'd last run my fingers through it. It swept into his eyes as he stepped into the bar and took in his surroundings. He was dressed for a night out in tight black jeans and a tight V-neck black T-shirt. Understated but hot. I noticed a few women and more than a couple men check him out. I wished I were at his side with the right to put a possessive arm around his waist. I wanted him to belong to me and for everyone to know it.

Jay and Peter were with him. They stood so much taller than him that it was hard not to notice them hovering over him protectively. And yes, they looked amazing too. Both men were wearing form-fitted dress shirts and designer jeans. Jay's jeans were faded, with strategically placed holes drawing the eye to... well, never mind. He looked sexy as hell. They were a strikingly handsome threesome.

I took a deep breath, tipped back the last of my vodka, and signaled to Sam. I was as ready as I'd ever be.

"Thank you, all! My buddy Matt is going to take over for a minute here. Matt, my man, take it away...."

The bar erupted in applause for Sam's performance and as a welcome for me. It was noisy, but somehow for me, at that moment, it was silent. It was like the night I first met Aaron at Club Indigo. The dance music had practically been vibrating through my body, but I had never been more aware of an undercurrent ripe with possibilities in the silence underneath the cacophony. The same soul-stopping awareness overcame me as I stepped up to the microphone to thank Sam and the audience. The difference was that I had to make my voice heard to one person and one person only underneath the clinking of glasses, the murmurs of drunken patrons, and the strings of my own guitar. I had to let Aaron know this song was meant for him alone.

I strummed a couple of chords and spoke clearly into the microphone, looking directly at Aaron. It was difficult to see him clearly in the darkened bar, but he looked agitated. I saw his expressive hands grasp on to Jay's arm almost as though he needed to be anchored. I wasn't sure what Peter or Jay had said to him to get him to come tonight, but Aaron certainly looked surprised to see me with a guitar in my hand in front of a modest audience. I couldn't worry about that now. He was here and that was all that mattered. I couldn't fuck this up.

"This song is one of my favorites. I can't always say the words I want to say or should say. So I'll say it in a song. This is for Aaron."

I cleared my throat and began the intro chords to Elton John's "Your Song." This would mean something to him. He would understand me when I sang.

My voice cracked at the line "yours are the sweetest eyes I've ever seen," but otherwise I made it through. I sang to him, willing him to understand the simplest message that just being with him was special, and I wanted him to be mine.

I strummed the song's final notes, and the crowd applauded wildly. I looked directly at Aaron, whose expression was difficult to see from the makeshift stage, and then stepped back to the microphone before Sam came to take over again. The song was over, but I had one last thing to say.

"Thank you. I love you, Aaron."

Aaron visibly jolted at the words and made a beeline for the exit. I hurriedly set my guitar on the stand nearest me and ran after him. People turned to see what the fuss was, but thankfully Sam had started a new set with a much livelier song than the one I'd left them with. They'd forget about me dodging tables and chairs to get to a fleeing audience member in no time.

I found him outside, leaning against the cool brick of the building's façade, looking breathless and upset. He bit his gloss-covered lip and closed his eyes when he heard me call his name.

"Aaron! I—"

Suddenly he was in my arms. He flung his body at me and I caught him, holding on as tightly as possible. I swayed him side to side, murmuring sweet nothings in his ear. I kissed his cheek, his neck, his jaw, his ears and eyes. I was a like a blind man who could see again. A drowning man who'd found safety on familiar shore at long last. Aaron gently pushed me back a step to look in my eyes. His own were wet with unshed tears, but there was a hopeful gaze there also. I'm not sure what he saw in mine, but I hoped he could see I meant every word I'd said. We stared a moment longer, and then our lips locked in a passionate kiss. Our tongues danced in a mating ritual of their own, tasting and licking and becoming one after a long absence.

Someone let out a wolf whistle on the sidewalk. I raised my right thumb in agreement, making Aaron break the kiss with a laugh.

"Idiot," he chided me with the sweetest expression. I wanted to know what he was trying to say with his eyes. We probably needed to sit down and have a real conversation, exploring with words what the meaning of all this was.

But not now. Now, I just wanted him. I kissed him again on his swollen lips and traced over the bottom one with my thumb.

"Baby, I want you. I've missed you… so much. Please. Come home with me?"

"With you? To your place? Don't you have roommates? We can go to mine. I… fuck, Matty. I…." His eyes pooled over and he sobbed in my arms. I held him tightly, shushing him and kissing his hair while I finally ran my fingers through it.

"My place is closer. Just a couple blocks away. I told my roommates about you. They know. Besides, it's eleven o'clock on a Saturday night. They won't be home anyway. Come on."

"Don't you need your guitar? I should tell Jay and Peter." He was softly crying in between words.

"Baby, don't cry. I'll get my guitar from Sam later. And don't worry about Jay and Peter. They'll know you're with me. Now come."

I pulled him along, shielding him in the cradle of my right arm as I led the way to my car.

The ride was silent and thankfully short.

"We're here. I can't find a closer parking spot."

Aaron didn't respond or look at me. I hoped he wasn't having second thoughts. I got out of the car and raced over to his side to open his door. He seemed surprised, but pleasantly so, at my chivalrous gesture. *Note to self: be more chivalrous.* I received the smile I'd been waiting for and felt my heart skip a beat. I led him up the street toward my building. I had no idea if Dave or Curt would be home. I was winging it when I told Aaron they wouldn't be. I hadn't thought quite that far ahead.

I started to feel a little panicky when I realized the place would probably be a mess. I'd straightened up a bit before I left because I needed to keep occupied, but even so, Aaron was a neat freak. I hoped Dave and Curt hadn't left beer bottles or other paraphernalia lying around. *Please be clean, please be clean.* I fiddled with the keys nervously as we stood at my door. Aaron gave me a shy, reassuring grin and it was all good again.

No one was home, thank God. I switched on the dimmest light possible and was relieved to find the place didn't look too shabby. Nowhere near as nice as Aaron's, but not bad.

"Want something to drink?" I offered, grabbing a couple water bottles.

"No, I'm good." He turned in a slow circle, taking in our small bachelor pad. "So, I finally see where Matt Sullivan lives."

"Um, yeah. It's not as nice as your place, but it's close to school and we can all afford it, so... it works." I took a swig from my water bottle, suddenly feeling nervous again.

"It's cool, Matt. No one home?"

"No, it doesn't look like it. Just so you know, I told them about us. About you. They want to meet you."

His face was a picture of astonishment. I gave a small laugh.

"Come on. My room is this way." I led him down the hall.

My bedroom was a decent size. Dave had commandeered the master bedroom, agreeing to pay more each month for the honor. Curt's and my rooms were roughly the same layout, and we shared a bathroom. Thankfully, Curt was relatively clean, so our arrangement had worked well. My bed was a queen-size and was pushed up against the window wall to make space for my desk. A dresser stood next to the desk with just a smidge of space left over for a small bookshelf and a nightstand next to the bed. I hung my two prize guitars on the wall and stored the cases in my closet. It was a little cramped, and nothing matched except the comforter cover and the pillows. And that was only because my mom had picked them out for me. I couldn't help but wonder what it looked like to Aaron. Student chic?

"So, this is it…," I said awkwardly, shoving my hands in my pockets.

"You have a lot of stuff." Aaron was looking at my law books and the clutter on my desk. "Looks important too."

He spotted a picture on my desk and picked it up for a closer look.

"Who are these people?"

"My family. That's my mom and dad, my brother Sean, my sister Shelly, and my younger twin sisters, Samantha and Sarah. I think that was taken at Christmas. I don't know. My mom snuck it in my bag as I was leaving. She's always assuming I'm a little homesick." I was babbling. *Shut up, Matt.* I could feel my face redden. I was hoping to get him in my bed, not bore him with family photos.

"This is us." He picked up the picture I'd had the paddleboat operator take of the two of us. It was very unlike me to do anything more than upload the occasional photo, but I really liked this one. It was a beautiful souvenir of a beautiful day. I couldn't resist making a hard copy for myself.

Aaron looked up at me with a sweet, teary-eyed grin.

"We look good together."

"We do, baby."

I sat on the edge of the bed, hoping he'd join me. He didn't disappoint. Aaron sat in my lap, and I huffed a breath of surprise as he tangled his arms around my neck. He looked deep into my eyes before touching his lips ever so softly to my own.

"Lock the door?"

I nodded, giving him a gentle shove so I could obey. I turned back to the bed to find Aaron sprawled out, looking oh so sexy dressed all in black against my dark-navy comforter.

"Matty, get naked. Please."

My hands shook as I fumbled with the buttons of my shirt. I threw it over my desk chair and started on my belt buckle, watching Aaron's expression. His eyes were filled with lust. He moved his right hand to cup his cock through his black jeans, stroking languidly. I swallowed.

"You too. Get naked. It's been too long, Aar. I need you."

I pulled my jeans off, and dressed only in my boxers, I covered his body with my own. I took his beautiful face in my hands and kissed him deeply, throwing all the passion racing through my blood into the connection. He moaned beneath me and began a slow writhing motion with his pelvis. I gasped as our hardened cocks touched for the first time in weeks. It felt so amazing, but I was now desperate to get us both naked. I slipped my hand under his T-shirt and pulled it up his chest, stopping to lick a line up his torso. I sucked his right nipple into my mouth and then traced slow circles around it before giving the same attention to his left nipple. I bit at him a little hard and licked him. He was writhing in earnest now, calling my name. I pulled his shirt over his head and went back to licking and kissing his chest while I worked on removing his belt and jeans. He lifted his hips off the bed as I slid his jeans over his ass. He wasn't wearing any boxers. I would have made a comment, but my mouth had gone dry.

My hands roamed over his ass cheeks, kneading and squeezing. His skin was so smooth and lovely; I was getting off just from touching him. I hadn't paid any attention to his gorgeous erect cock yet, and he was getting impatient, if the moans and sway of his hips were any indication. I laughed softly, and keeping one hand on his right ass cheek, I used my free hand to gently take hold of his dick. He gasped out loud, opened his eyes, and propped himself on his elbows to watch me. I had never sucked him off. I'd topped him each time we'd had sex. He said he preferred bottoming, and I wasn't sure I was ready for that anyway. But he'd sucked my cock many a time. Hell, he had done it well before I'd been inside him for the first time, months ago. I was nervous to be on the giving end of a blow job, but I figured I needed to get over that fast. What guy doesn't like having his dick sucked? I wanted to do this for Aaron. I probably would suck at it (pun intended), but practice makes perfect, right?

I held him a little tighter, watching the precum puddle at the tip. His cock was darker in color than my own, and he kept the hair around his penis trimmed. His balls were practically hairless. He'd told me before that manscaping was vital. Well, it looked pretty fucking fantastic to me. I breathed in his scent before placing a small teasing kiss on the tip. Then I licked the broad head and twirled my tongue around it experimentally. I tasted the precum and made a "yum" sound. Aaron closed his eyes and threw his head back. So far, so good.

I freed my hand from under his ass and massaged his balls as I licked his gorgeous cock from base to tip. I did it a few times, testing out different angles before taking as much as I could of his rock-hard member into my mouth. I sucked and licked, thinking I should just do what I liked and hopefully Aaron would like it too. He did. He gazed at me through hooded eyes while licking his own lips in appreciation. After a few minutes, he placed a hand on my head to still my movement.

"Stop. Fuck! You have no idea how sexy that is, honey. Matty, you are so fucking hot."

He leaned down to kiss me. He was all heat and energy now. He was practically vibrating with desire. My own dick was fighting to get out of the confines of my boxer shorts. They were wet in the front from the judicious leaking coming from my own overexcited state. Aaron pushed them over my ass and went straight to work on my cock. I kneeled on the bed as he pushed himself on his stomach, facing me with his perfect ass straight in the air. I leaned over to cup his ass as he sucked and licked me over and over.

It was beyond sexy, but I didn't want to come this way. I wanted inside him.

"Baby, can I… let me inside you, please."

Aaron got up on his knees facing me, and nodded eagerly as he pulled the comforter back.

"How do you want me?" His voice sounded so soft in the quiet room.

"I want to look at you."

I rummaged for supplies in my nightstand and turned back to the bed to find him lying, naked, with his arms held out in welcome. So gorgeous.

I crawled between his thighs, and after pouring a little lube in my hand, I slowly stretched his opening with one finger. I added a second finger while I stroked his cock with my left hand.

"Oh fuck, Matty. I'm ready. Come on. Fuck me."

My breath was coming in shortened pants. I struggled to steady my hands to get the condom unwrapped. Aaron laughed and sat up, grabbing the condom from me. He unwrapped it and slid it over my very erect member. I sighed at the feel of his touch. He lay back and held his knees up in invitation. I held my breath to steady my nerves before adding a little more lube to the condom. Then I placed my cock at his entrance and slowly made my way inside my lover.

It was heaven. Absolute nirvana. I knew I wouldn't last this time. It had been too long since we'd been intimate, and my body was crying with relief at finally being joined with Aaron's. He was so tight. I made a painstaking effort to go slow so as not to hurt him. I could feel the sweat on my forehead. I looked down at him to make sure he was okay. When I was fully enveloped by his hot channel, I stilled myself to await his signal. I was shaky, but managed to stave off the desire to plunge into him over and over. He didn't make me wait long. A short nod told me to move. I gently retreated and then moved inside him. We both moaned with pleasure. Nothing had ever felt so good, so right. I moved slowly inside him, savoring the feel of his body around mine. Aaron elevated his hips to meet my thrust. He cried out as I hit his gland. I couldn't contain myself any longer. All the frustration and joy of finally having him in my arms again rushed through my body. I fucked him hard and fast, sweat bathing both of us as we clung to one another in ecstasy. Aaron cried my name again and pulled at my hair hard when he came. I kept up my pace, riding him through the waves of orgasm before finally succumbing to my own.

I collapsed on Aaron's much smaller body. He wrapped his arms around me tightly in a sweet embrace before I could tell my weight was too much for him. Panting as though I'd just run a marathon, I carefully disengaged our bodies and set about disposing of the condom and cleaning up my man. Aaron watched me through hooded, sleepy eyes, with a soft smile on his beautiful mouth. I kissed his lips as I joined him back in bed, tucked him in the cradle of my arms, and pulled the comforter back over us.

Aaron burrowed into my side, with his cheek pressed against my heart. He was exactly where he was supposed to be. As if in unspoken agreement, we both drifted to sleep, knowing the morning would force us to deal with reality. Tonight, no words were necessary.

I AWOKE the next morning to the sweet sound of Aaron's soft snoring. He always denied he was a snorer, but truthfully, I found it adorable. His face was squished on the pillow, and both of his hands rested under his cheek. He resembled a sleeping angel. I stared for a few quiet moments before my bladder demanded attention. I slipped on some pajama bottoms before heading for the bathroom, then made my way to the kitchen to start some coffee, since I was up already. Curt had beat me to it. He was leaning against the kitchen counter, staring bleary eyed at the coffee maker.

"Mornin'," he mumbled.

I mumbled my own greeting to him before grabbing two mugs and setting them next to the one he had placed for himself next to the machine. Curt noticed the third mug and waggled his eyebrows suggestively.

"So… do you have a guest over?"

"Yeah." I couldn't contain my smile. I was more than a little pleased to wake up with Aaron in bed beside me again.

"Everything good, then?"

"Yeah. We'll have to talk things through, I guess, but yeah… he's here and that's really good. You did make enough, right?" I tilted my head toward the coffee pot. Too much talking in the morning before coffee wasn't my thing. I needed something to clear the cobwebs away.

"Sure. There should be enough, Casanova. Help yourself."

I took the two mugs of coffee back to my room, where Aaron was stretched out with his arms resting above his head. He looked like an underwear model, minus the underwear.

"Hmm… morning, Matty. Coffee for me?" He shifted to lie on his side, propped up by his elbow as I moved to set the coffee on my nightstand. I kissed his forehead and nose before pulling back to take a good look at him.

"Of course. Curt's up. He made it, so if it sucks, don't think badly of me."

He laughed and eased himself to a sitting position. I bit back the urge to ask if I'd hurt him last night. He would roll his eyes at me, and I didn't want to take anything away from the experience. Last night was incredible. *Leave it alone, Matt.*

"Not bad."

I took a sip of mine, peering at him over the edge of the coffee mug. One of us was going to have to bring up the subject of "us." If we wanted this to work, we had to deal with some things. I understood that; however, I was loath to lose the easy feeling of sipping coffee with my naked lover on a Sunday morning.

"You okay?" Aaron asked me in a puzzled tone.

"Better than...." I borrowed his line from months ago, after the first night we'd made love. He understood and smiled sweetly.

"We need to talk." Aaron set his coffee aside and turned back to face me with a laugh. "You don't need to look so gloomy, Matty. I just think that—"

I leaned over to quiet him with a kiss. I was relieved he knew we needed to address our relationship, if we were to have one, but there was an equal part of me that was scared shitless about the impending conversation.

"Sorry. I didn't mean to interrupt. I just have to tell you that I... I want this, Aaron. I want you. I want us to be together. I'm no good at saying this kind of stuff, so if I fuck it up, please just know that that is what I care about."

Aaron shot me one of those patient stares that told me I was a little on the dramatic side, but he was going to let it slide for now.

"You say you want us, Matt. I do too. But you've never been with a man before in a relationship. Are you saying you want to be boyfriends? Or is the concept too weird to you? I'm not trying to make you uncomfortable, but I need to know some basic things here."

"Yes. I want you to be my boyfriend."

Fuck, that sounded so high school. My voice squeaked at the "boyfriend" word, but I meant it. I wanted us to be a couple.

"Okay, me too. What does that mean to you, exactly?"

He took pity on me when I stared blankly at him. I hadn't had enough coffee yet.

"I mean, do you want to date other people? Because I'm going to be honest with you, I—"

I put my hand over his mouth.

"No. I'm not sharing. I don't share. I can't 'date' you casually. Aaron…."

I took a deep breath, put my hands on his shoulders, and looked him directly in his gorgeous eyes. "I love you."

He looked as overwhelmed by those words this morning as he had last night. Maybe this was too much too soon, but I wouldn't take them back even if I could. I could only hope that maybe he would one day return them. I didn't mind waiting as long as I had him by my side.

"Matt. You don't know if you really l—"

"Don't fucking say that to me. I know how I feel. And yes, it may be hard for you to believe it, but Aaron, I mean it. I have never felt this way about anyone else. And I don't want to share you. I want us to be together as often as possible. I want to talk to you or text and e-mail you when we can't be together. I want to be the first person you want to talk to when you're really excited about something or even if you're really sad." I took a breath, afraid I just sounded corny as hell. "I'm sorry I gave you reason to doubt me, but I want another chance."

"Okay."

"Okay? That's it? What's the catch?"

"No catch. I don't want to share you either. I want us. I want a relationship with you and all that entails. But I have to admit something, Matt." He looked out the window before turning to face me again. His expression was so vulnerable.

"What, baby?"

"I'm afraid. I'm afraid that you'll decide you want to be with a woman. That you want a wife, kids, dog, house in the suburbs... things I can't give you. Well, I guess I could do the dog, but not the others. Those other things are normal and expected, and it's a lifestyle you always thought you'd have. Are you sure you want me instead?"

This was important. I knew my answer mattered. I had to be honest but still let him know where I was coming from.

"Will you listen to me? Really listen. Because this is probably one of those times I could fuck up without meaning to." Aaron nodded cautiously. "I don't want a woman or another man. I only want you. Neither of us knows what the future holds, but when I think about the future, I want you in mine. Remember when you said that there are no guarantees, but you want something that feels like the real thing. You are that to me."

Aaron's eyes watered over, and he swiped at falling tears with the back of his hand. I grabbed his hand in mine and kissed it.

"The rest we take one day at a time, okay? I don't want a wife, kids, and dog with a house in the suburbs tomorrow." He shot me an angry look and scooted away from me. I grabbed him back and pulled him onto my lap, tickling his side.

"What I mean is that I don't want any of those things right away and.... Listen! Are you listening?" He nodded slowly, still not looking at me. "Who's to say it can't be a husband, kids, dog, and an apartment in the city?"

Aaron met my eyes.

"You mean that?"

"Yes. I really mean that."

"Oh, Matty...." He buried his face in my shoulder and held on tightly. I rocked him in my arms, feeling so grateful to have this amazing chance. This amazing man. I wanted to lay him back in my bed and make love to him all morning. And then, later, I'd introduce my boyfriend to my friends.

This was definitely better than good.

LANE HAYES is a designer by trade, but is first and foremost a lover of the written word. An avid reader from an early age, Lane has always been drawn to romance novels. She truly believes there is nothing more inspiring than a well-told love story. Lane discovered the M/M genre a few years ago and was instantly hooked. She loves to travel and wishes she could do it more often. Lane lives in Southern California with her amazing husband, three teenage kids, and Rex, the coolest yellow lab ever.

E-mail Lane at lanehayes@ymail.com.

STAINED GLASS
Jaime Samms

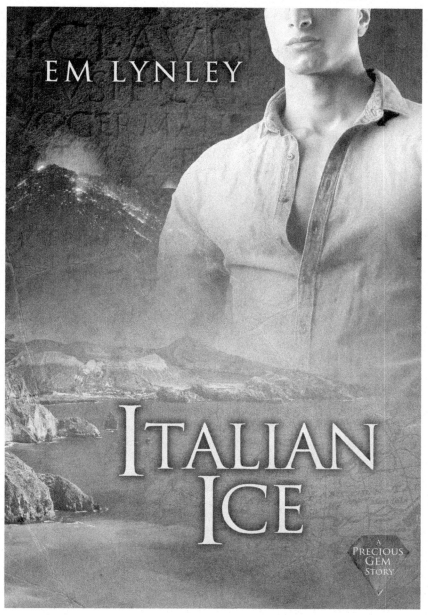

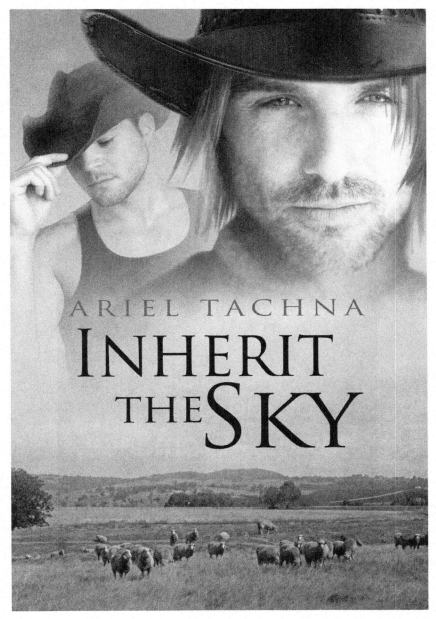

CPSIA information can be obtained at www.ICGtesting.com
Printed in the USA
BVOW05s2348030916

461012BV00009B/317/P

9 781623 806392